"How did you find me?" Lisa asked, hardly daring to believe that Pete was really there in her office.

"I called you at home and there was no answer. I took a chance you might be working late, strolled by, saw a light on, and . . ." Pete gazed down at Lisa's parted lips and forgot what he was saying. Breathing deeply, drinking in the elusive scent of her perfume, a subtle blend of musk and exotic flowers that had haunted him at random moments since the night they'd met in New Orleans, he felt his pulse start to race like a teenager's souped-up Chevy careening out of control.

Lisa knew she had to defuse the moment. She mustn't give in to the powerful feelings Pete was stirring in her. She flattened her hands on his chest, meaning to push him away gently. But her resolve was no match for her desire, as she felt the wild hammering of Pete's heart and saw the sudden purpose in his mesmerizing blue eyes. And when he brushed his mouth across hers in a lingering caress, she simply melted against him. . . .

WHAT ARE *LOVESWEPT* ROMANCES?

They are stories of true romance and touching emotion. We believe those two very important ingredients are constants in our highly sensual and very believable stories in the *LOVESWEPT* line. Our goal is to give you, the reader, stories of consistently high quality that may sometimes make you laugh, sometimes make you cry, but are always fresh and creative and contain many delightful surprises within their pages.

Most romance fans read an enormous number of books. Those they truly love, they keep. Others may be traded with friends and soon forgotten. We hope that each *LOVESWEPT* romance will be a treasure—a "keeper." We will always try to publish

LOVE STORIES YOU'LL NEVER FORGET
BY AUTHORS YOU'LL ALWAYS REMEMBER

The Editors

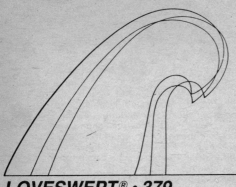

LOVESWEPT® • 379

Gail Douglas
The Dreamweavers:
Sophisticated Lady

 BANTAM BOOKS
NEW YORK • TORONTO • LONDON • SYDNEY • AUCKLAND

SOPHISTICATED LADY

A Bantam Book / February 1990

*LOVESWEPT® and the wave device are registered
trademarks of Bantam Books, a division of
Bantam Doubleday Dell Publishing Group, Inc.
Registered in U.S. Patent
and Trademark Office and elsewhere.*

*If you would be interested in receiving protective vinyl
covers for your Loveswept books, please write to this address
for information:*

*Loveswept
Bantam Books
P.O. Box 985
Hicksville, NY 11802*

ISBN 0-553-44013-6

Published simultaneously in the United States and Canada

*Bantam Books are published by Bantam Books, a division
of Bantam Doubleday Dell Publishing Group, Inc. Its trademark, consisting of the words "Bantam Books" and the
portrayal of a rooster, is Registered in U.S. Patent and
Trademark Office and in other countries. Marca Registrada.
Bantam Books, 666 Fifth Avenue, New York, New York 10103.*

PRINTED IN THE UNITED STATES OF AMERICA

O   0 9 8 7 6 5 4 3 2 1

TO ENID
Having a wonderful time; wish you were here.

One

Pete Cochrane's "A-Train" nearly got derailed.

Rolling along without a care, Pete had glanced up from the keyboard into enormous, almond-shaped, smoky eyes, and for perhaps the first time in his career, he'd missed a beat. Or his heart had.

He was shocked. Where were the intricate phrasings of his tribute to Duke Ellington? The playful shooby-doo-wah riffs? The dancing left-hand runs?

Pete struggled to regain his equilibrium. It wasn't easy. He was too captivated by the honey blond across the room to think about keyboard counterpoint. For a while longer, he had to let his disciplined fingers carry on as best they could.

Poised just inside the Bourbon Street club's entrance, the woman was a shimmer of pale gold in the dim room, as if bathed in the circle of her own spotlight.

Pete told himself he shouldn't be all that attracted to her. She looked too remote. Untouchable. Unreachable. Besides, he's learned a long time ago to avoid entanglements at the clubs where he played.

But those eyes . . .

Pete's glance moved slowly over the luminous vision. He liked the blond hair. It was stylish. Classy. Cut in a sort of twenties bob, side-parted, thick, and loosely waved, it was a perfect frame for her delicate features.

The mouth gave him pause. Full lips tinted the pale pink shade of the inside of a seashell were slightly parted and curved in a tiny smile. Pete's gaze caressed their velvety softness for several seconds.

Then the eyes captivated him again. The puzzled expression in them brought him up short: Could this lady possibly be aware that he wasn't doing the Ellington number the way he should? Was she familiar with his style?

He harnessed his concentration. After a few successfully inventive measures, he glanced up in time to be rewarded by a knowing smile, and though his fingers somehow kept a steady rhythm, his pulse launched into a syncopation all its own. The woman *did* know his work. Amazing. He was used to flirtatious females. He wasn't accustomed to silent, savvy critiques from them.

Pete felt as if she'd given him an unexpected gift. It called for some tribute in return, some special song just for her. But what?

Noting again the slim figure, the understated elegance of the short, body-skimming, shoulder-baring black dress that looked as if it bore a very good designer label, the shapely legs enhanced by sheer black silk, the slender feet in delicate sandals, Pete needed no more inspiration.

While he segued from one Ellington number to another, slowing the pace to an easy, restrained version of "Sophisticated Lady," he met the mesmerizing gaze again and held it steadily until, just to be sure there was no doubt of his message, he grinned and winked—all the while wondering why he was bending his long-standing rule about mixing women and work.

His smile faded as an annoyingly good-looking man beside the blond bent down to whisper something in her ear.

Pete realized he'd been so wrapped up in the woman, he hadn't noticed she was with several other people.

When it hit him that he was feeling a sharp pang of possessiveness toward someone he didn't even know, he couldn't fathom what was going on inside him. He was thirty-four, not nineteen. A hardened veteran of the battleground of fleeting romance, not a wide-eyed new recruit. Though he wasn't immune to beautiful females, he wasn't all that susceptible to them either. He just didn't grant them much importance in his scheme of things. Not anymore. So what could explain their locked gazes and his rollicking heartbeat?

Lisa Sinclair was asking herself the same question as Justin Fuller's tug on her arm slowly brought her out of a trance. Blinking, she finally nodded and managed to follow Justin and the rest of their party toward a table one of them had spotted.

Spying an old friend, Lisa excused herself from her little group to take a brief detour. "Hi," she said with a smile, thrusting out her hand as Harry Milton started to rise. "Don't get up," she added hastily. "It's too crowded to try." Besides, she thought, she didn't want to stand around visiting for too long. Although she liked Harry and wouldn't have dreamed of going past him without stopping to say hello, she was eager to get to her table, sit down, and collect her senses. It wasn't at all like her to gape at a performer the way she'd stared at Pete Cochrane. Groupies did that sort of thing. Follow-the-band types. Not Lisa Sinclair.

Harry resettled his large frame into his chair. "It's good to see you on this side of the Atlantic, Lisa. Are you in town for a while?"

"I'm heading back to Nice tomorrow," she answered with a smile. "I expect I'll be seeing you there shortly as well, won't I? The festival is shaping up to be one of the best ever."

"Well, for my money, the Nice jazzfest beats them all," Harry said, then added with a grin, "Have you heard that I'm going over in Jack Bakersfield's place?"

"No, but I'm not surprised," Lisa said, pleased for Harry. "Someone said Jack was involved in a minor car accident. He's okay, isn't he?"

"Jack's on the mend. and he's a good enough sport to thank me for sitting in for him. I don't even have to feel guilty about going to the Riviera to play in his band while he's stuck at home with his leg in a cast. By the way, now that our youngest is in college, I finally talked my better half into coming with me."

"Terrific," Lisa said sincerely. "It'll be Sheila's first time in Nice, won't it? She must be excited."

Harry nodded, chuckling. "She's already packed her new bikini. Looks darn good in it too," he said proudly, then added, "We're going to stay on for a while after the festival. For as long as a month, if we like it. It'll be kind of a second honeymoon."

Lisa felt a rush of affection for the balding, slightly overweight drummer whose down-to-earth decency almost made her believe it was possible for a professional musician to lead a normal life, to fall in love and stay there, even to be a family man. "You'll have a great time," she said with genuine warmth. "I'm sure we'll run into each other at some point at the festival, but if not, give me a call if you have time. We can have a drink together, at least. And incidentally, Jack Bakersfield *should* be grateful that you're available, Harry. You're the best in the business. His band is lucky to have you."

Harry's brown eyes twinkled, deep laugh lines forming at the corners as he grinned, clearly pleased by Lisa's compliment. "I'll tell the guys what you said. Maybe they'll give me a little respect for a change."

"Harry Milton, the Rodney Dangerfield of Bourbon Street," Lisa teased, deciding it was time to rejoin her group and sit down. She couldn't endure another second of Pete Cochrane's unwavering gaze. "I'd better catch up with my friends before somebody steals my place, Harry. Give Sheila my best."

"Will we see you at that little club where I caught up with you last year?" Harry called after her as she moved away.

"Probably," Lisa answered. A moment later, lowering herself into the chair that had been saved for her, she realized with a start that she was directly facing Pete Cochrane. And he was still looking at her, not even trying to be subtle about it.

Obviously she'd given him the wrong impression by staring at him, she thought, refusing to take so much as one more glance at his rugged, handsome face and the athletic build that was evident under his impeccably tailored tuxedo.

Never having seen a photograph of Pete Cochrane, she hadn't known what to expect when curiosity had compelled her to come to hear him in person.

She'd chosen to imagine a cerebral type, thin and intense with black horn-rimmed glasses—a kind of uptown Buddy Holly.

He looked more like James Bond. She'd been afraid of just that possibility. She'd wanted him to be unthreateningly bland.

But with his dark hair and straight, heavy brows, his strong features and muscular body, he exuded a potent masculinity that made the sounds he created and the emotions he evoked all the more exciting, the gentle cadences suddenly charged with an undercurrent of restrained power.

Lisa hadn't been prepared to encounter such a virile man. His album cover hadn't given her a clue, what with its soft-focus photograph of a single red rose tossed carelessly on a keyboard.

From the corner of her eye, Lisa saw a voluptuous redhead slither over to the piano bar and onto the stool closest to Pete Cochrane, her smile predatory, her overflowing curves battling to escape the inadequate confines of a yellow knit dress.

Aware of an idiotic flutter in the pit of her stomach that felt suspiciously like jealousy, Lisa firmly told herself she should be glad that a rival for Mr. Cochrane's attention had arrived on the scene.

"What are you having, Lisa?" Justin asked.

Lisa turned and stared blankly at him for several long seconds before answering. "A white wine spritzer, please," she said at last, uncomfortably aware that her vagueness was arousing Justin's curiosity.

Justin's fiancée leaned forward to peer around him at Lisa. "The word is that wine spritzers are out of fashion these days," Roberta Langley said, her blue eyes sparkling as she poked fun at Lisa's life among the international set.

Lisa smiled good-naturedly, grateful for her friend's frivolous distraction. "Sorry, Bobby-Jo. Have I tarnished my with-it image?"

"Well, yes, as a matter of fact. There you are, living on the Riviera, and yet you obviously don't keep up with what's hot and what's not among the rich and famous. I get more inside dope from Robin Leach than from you, Lisa Sinclair. You don't appreciate the chic life. I'll tell you what: You come back to New Orleans and run my bookshop while I go hobnob with your ritzy crowd in the south of France."

"Don't tempt me, Bobby-Jo," Lisa said.

Justin cocked his head to one side. "You mean you're not happy with your life?"

"Has anyone mentioned your tendency to overstatement, Justin?" Lisa asked with a grin. She knew he'd sensed her tension and was misreading it. If only she could stop feeling as if Pete Cochrane were watching her every gesture, she thought with a rush of irritation, she might not be so edgy. What gave the man the right to subject her to such bold scrutiny? Granted, he probably thought she'd been coming on to him, but she'd been careful not to look at him again after her initial double take. Why couldn't he choose a likelier object for his attention? He couldn't lack for volunteers. Not with his looks.

"I mean it, Lisa," Justin said. "Is living in Europe beginning to lose its charm?"

Lisa answered carefully, trying to be honest. "I'm enjoying every minute of living there, but I do miss New Orleans. It's the nearest thing to a hometown I've ever had. It also has the special attraction of my sister and brother-in-law, as well as you two, so of course I wish I could come back more often. Maybe even permanently, one of these days."

"How *is* your big sister?" Roberta asked. "Is Stefanie happy to be with T.J. again? Not that I can imagine how anyone wouldn't be. He's such a honey."

Lisa laughed. "Isn't he, though? And the two of them finally seem to have figured out the art of compromise, thank heavens. They're doing just fine."

"That's good news," Roberta said, then turned to join in an animated conversation with her other friends.

Justin spoke quietly to Lisa. "So all men aren't creeps?"

"Have I ever suggested they were?" Lisa said with real surprise. "I adore my father, I'm crazy about T.J. and my other brother-in-law, Cole, and . . ." She winked at Justin. "Even you can be bearable if you work at it. So why would I speak ill of your gender?"

He ignored the gibe. "How about this piano player? Is he a creep?"

The trouble with old college buddies, Lisa thought, was that they knew a person too well. Justin had picked up on the invisible but palpable sparks coming from the direction of the piano—and, whether she liked it or not, emanating from her as well. She shrugged, pretending nonchalance. "Who knows?"

Justin folded his arms on the table and studied Lisa intently. "You could find out if you wanted to. The man's taken with you. He can't keep his eyes off you. And I saw the way you ogled him when we came into this club."

"I did not ogle," Lisa said huffily, then chewed on her lip. "Tell me I didn't ogle, Justin."

"For once in your life, why don't you take a chance on a guy?" Justin answered. "Encourage him a little. You've raved about Pete Cochrane for months.

Here's your big moment. Are you going to let it pass you by?"

Lisa decided to treat the matter lightly. "Hey, Justin, I'm leaving in the morning for France, remember? A one-night fling, even with Pete Cochrane, doesn't appeal to me. I don't play those games. And I've been raving about his *music*. I don't know the man. I don't intend to know him. He's attractive, but I'm not interested."

"You know, if you weren't a Sinclair, I'd think you were running scared because you'd been burned by some whistling gypsy," Justin said.

Lisa swallowed hard but made herself keep smiling so Justin wouldn't guess that his blind shot had hit the bull's-eye. "But I *am* a Sinclair," she said with a lift of her chin. "Now, why don't we just relax and listen to the music? That's what we came for, right?"

"Cochrane's not playing now," Justin shot back. "He's checking his requests."

Lisa realized that Justin was right. The music had stopped.

She couldn't resist a casual glance. Pete Cochrane wasn't staring at her anymore. He was unfolding and reading the crumpled notes and scribbled-on coasters the waiter had left beside him on the piano bar. She felt oddly bereft. Had the man lost interest in her already? Typical, she thought, then laughed silently at her perversity. One saxophone player's not-so-merry chase had left one Lisa Sinclair jaded and utterly unreasonable.

Her amusement faded as she saw that the redhead at the piano bar—who looked rather like an overripe banana aching to be peeled—was trying in vain to engage the pianist in conversation. The poor thing was getting nothing more than polite responses for her trouble, Lisa noticed.

It occurred to Lisa that she was the one doing the staring now. And was she usually so catty? An overripe banana? How unkind. How nasty. How apt, she thought wickedly.

"You're not interested, huh?" Justin said, his lips twitching with laughter. "Which of your nine lives would you like to bet on it?" When Lisa narrowed her almond-shaped eyes, and Pete Cochrane started playing again, Justin backed off. "Okay, Lisa. Listen to your music. But don't come crying to me when you're a lonely old maid with nothing but a few worn-out records to fill your empty nights."

Lisa laughed. She'd always loved Justin's melodramatic flair. But as he turned to chat with the others, she stared at the back of his blond head for a moment, stunned at how accurate he'd been with every one of his comments.

Even as she listened to the persuasive piano stylings she knew so well, she was transported back to her apartment in Nice where that very music had become her favorite companion. It was the perfect lover: abstract, invisible, and safe.

Soon Lisa was lost in a smooth Gershwin tune that flowed over her like honey. Settling back in her chair, she became oblivious of everything but the seductive melodies, closing her eyes to savor them to the fullest.

Watching her, Pete was enchanted. This cool, self-possessed woman wasn't just listening to his music. She was giving herself to it. To him.

He was caught up in a strange, disturbingly sensual encounter, playing every note for just one person, unashamedly spinning out romantic ballads that spoke of hearts standing still and strangers across crowded rooms and sweet, comic valentines.

Lisa almost imagined she could feel the lightness of his touch on her skin as his fingers toyed and flirted and danced with the piano keys, and when the mood changed and his touch intensified to a deep caress of each separate note, the passion restrained but powerful, Lisa felt the quiver of sympathetic vibrations deep within her, heating her blood and matching her pulse and heartbeat to his rhythms.

As he ended the set with the liquid strains of "Easy to Love," Lisa opened her eyes to meet his penetrating gaze. He played a final, provocative chord that somehow left a suggestion of much, much more to be explored, then touched a finger to one last sensual note, watching Lisa as the sound slowly faded.

He got to his feet, still looking at her.

Lisa's skin burned. Her heart raced. How could a man make her feel so much without a word or a touch? How could she respond with such abandon?

Marshaling her weakened forces of resistance, she desperately tuned in on the conversation swirling around her and tried to ignore Pete Cochrane.

Pete was confused by her sudden withdrawal. Why had she turned away from him? Why was she trying to deny what was happening? Was she playing some game with him?

"Can y'all play 'Georgia'?" the redhead on the bar stool piped up. "That's where I'm from. A li'l ol' Georgia peach, that's me."

Pete gave her a practiced smile. He'd spent some time in Georgia. The redhead's accent didn't match any he'd heard there. He wondered why people tried to pretend to be what they weren't. " 'Georgia'? Sure.

Great number," he said politely. "I'll play it right after my break."

"Aw, aren't y'all just a honey? Now, how 'bout joinin' me for a li'l ol' drinkie-pooh?"

"Thanks, but I can't," Pete said, suppressing a wince and doing his best to sound regretful. Dealing with would-be playmates was a part of the job he wasn't crazy about, but he'd mastered the techniques early in his career. He was a musician, not an escort service. "There are some people I have to talk to," he said with as pleasant a smile as he could muster, then left the piano and gently but effectively scythed a path through the crowd, straight to his goal. "Hi," he said with a more genuine but slightly guarded smile as his honey blond stared up at him, obviously taken aback by the directness of his approach.

"Hi," she answered, her voice hardly more than a whisper.

Pete was surprised by his own aggressiveness. It wasn't like him to walk up to a strange woman anywhere and speak to her, much less in a club when he was on the job. But in this case, with this woman, he made an exception—and he wasn't sure why. "Hi," he said again, then cleared his throat. "I want to thank you."

"To thank me?" she repeated, her huge eyes wider than ever.

Pete lost himself in those eyes again. And in the sound of her voice. It was low and lovely and as soft as old velvet. "It isn't often I have such a good listener," he explained with a smile directed only at her. He didn't care about the curious glances of her companions. "And you knew I was cheating on 'A-Train.' Not many people would."

"I . . . I'm familiar with your work," Lisa explained,

shaken by the unexpected encounter, a dangerous flame inside her fanned by the nearness of Pete Cochrane's muscular body and the steadiness of his gaze. She had to struggle to keep a tremor out of her voice. "I have your album," she added, feeling the need to explain why she would notice every nuance of his style.

"So you're the one who bought it," Pete said with a touch of self-deprecation. He noted that the lady wore no ring on the all-important third finger, left hand. But there were other jewels: priceless emeralds subtly buried in the charcoal depths of her eyes. "May I buy a round of drinks for you and your friends?" he suggested impulsively, hoping his offer would earn him an invitation to sit down even though it was against his better judgment.

The ploy worked. And everyone shuffled to make room for Pete to pull up a chair right where he wanted to be—beside her. He decided that such co-operation meant she couldn't be attached to any of the men in her little group of friends.

She was even more enchanting up close, he thought, resisting an insane urge to brush the backs of his fingers over her pale, perfect skin, to capture her full lower lip between his teeth and gently nibble on it.

Lisa experienced the same waves of sensation he'd created in her with his playing, the mere expression in his blue eyes now arousing her to giddy heights. Yet she felt awkward with him after the intimate secrets they'd just shared. It was like waking up with a lover after a night of revealing tender vulnerabilities.

She had to look away. The erotic tension was too much.

But her gaze rested on the strong hands that were loosely, casually clasped on the table, and another rush of excitement coursed through her. She kept thinking of the magic Pete's long, capable fingers could perform, her imagination tantalizing her without mercy.

Taking a deep breath to steady herself, Lisa found her body suddenly infused with a crisp male scent, intoxicating and delicious. It seemed that nothing she tried would work to diminish the man's impact on her. It was a conspiracy of the senses.

She was grateful to Justin for choosing that moment to make introductions all around. But the second after he'd done the honors, he turned away again to talk to the rest of the group—deliberately, she suspected—leaving her to fend for herself with Pete Cochrane.

"Lisa Sinclair," Pete said, quietly repeating her name as if deciding whether it suited her. He motioned to the waiter to take orders for the whole table and put it on his tab, then smiled at her.

And Lisa knew with an unnerving certainty that her perfect lover had ceased to be abstract, or invisible—or safe.

Two

"What's your poison?" Justin asked when the waiter had taken the orders for everyone at the table but Pete and Lisa.

Pete's gaze remained on Lisa. "Bourbon on the rocks," he answered, just to be polite. He didn't care what they put in his glass. All he wanted to drink in was Lisa Sinclair.

"How about you, squirt?" Justin said. "Another spritzer?"

"Nothing more for me, thanks," she said, indicating her half-full glass.

"I owe you one, then," Pete said to her in a low voice. His smile broadened, and he raised one dark brow questioningly as he realized what Justin had called this exquisite, regal creature. "*Squirt?*"

Lisa laughed, embarrassed but glad of the chance to initiate some small talk. "Justin's been a friend for too long, I'm afraid. He picked up the nickname from my three sisters. I'm five-six, but they're all taller, and two of them are older, so I've been squirt for as long as I can remember, and probably will be forever."

Pete enjoyed her laughter, a sparkling sound that reminded him of good champagne. He liked the way the green crystals in her eyes glinted with humor, the way her smile lit up her face. Rapidly he was adjusting his original impression that she was some remote, untouchable creature. She was very touchable. "Are you from New Orleans?" he asked, going straight to the basics. He couldn't afford to indulge in trivial preliminaries. He had to find out all he could about Lisa Sinclair before his break ended.

She shook her head. "Not really. I spend as many chunks of time here as I can, though. New Orleans is my home base, if not my hometown."

"And the chunks when you're not here? Where are you then?"

"Mostly in France," she answered, absently doodling in the moisture on the outside of her glass with the perfectly manicured tip of her index finger. "In fact, I'll be back in Nice by this time tomorrow night." There, she thought. She'd said it. Pete Cochrane now knew how things stood. And though she had to admit she felt oddly cheated by the fact that this tenuous beginning would lead nowhere, she hoped the man's apparent interest in her would end. If not, it would be painfully clear that all he was looking for was a one-nighter.

At the suggestion of finality in Lisa's voice, Pete suppressed a smile. He'd been looking forward to Nice for weeks, ever since Harry Milton had talked him into going to the jazz festival there. It was a happy coincidence that Harry seemed to be acquainted with Lisa, would probably even know where to find her in Nice.

Life at its best was like music at its best, Pete mused. Full of unanticipated grace notes.

But for the moment, he chose not to mention his plans to attend the festival; Lisa might not be the least bit interested. "So you live in France," he said instead. "Now I understand why you have my album. I sell better there than here."

"That's quite an understatement," Lisa said, wishing she didn't sound quite so breathless. "You're a big hit where I live."

Pete laughed in surprise. "A big hit?" he repeated, then felt the heat of a flush rising over his cheeks. Still a hick inside, he thought with a few mental curses. He wondered sometimes why he was striving so hard for success. When any hint of it came his way, he felt like a fumbling adolescent, unsure how to deal with it, unable even to take a compliment. "So what do you do in Nice, Lisa?" he asked.

Lisa didn't know what to make of Pete's sudden awkwardness. And was he actually blushing a little? She'd spent a lot of time around musicians. Blushing wasn't common to the breed. Neither was modesty. Perhaps Pete Cochrane simply had the humble bit down pat. "I'm in travel," she answered.

"Travel," Pete echoed, wondering about the vague statement. She could be anything from a ticket agent to an idle jet-setter.

Justin leaned toward them long enough to add his contribution. "Lisa won't tell you herself, but she's a Dreamweaver."

"I can believe that," Pete murmured with a meaningful glance at Lisa. He turned briefly to Justin, feeling uncommonly friendly toward the younger man, who was acting very much like a none-too-subtle matchmaker. "Exactly what is a dreamweaver?"

"Dreamweavers, Inc.," Justin said. "It's a tour company with flair. Lisa and her three sisters operate it. They named it after the *Dreamweaver*, their parents' boat." Having imparted that bit of vital information, Justin went back to chatting with Roberta and the others.

Pete looked at Lisa with increased interest. The one possibility he hadn't thought of was that she might be a successful international businesswoman. "Come to think of it, I'm familiar with your firm," he said as a few small pieces of knowledge began fitting together in his mind. "I've seen your advertisements, and I've been on a riverboat that was a Dreamweavers operation. I was giving some out-of-town friends a fifty-cent tour of The Big Easy, and I took them on a *Bayou Belle* dinner cruise. It was terrific. Flawless. I was so impressed, I helped myself to some of the literature on your other operations—and even read it."

"The *Bayou Belle* is Stefanie's boat," Lisa said, unable to suppress a smile of pride for the company she and her sisters had created. "Steffie's my oldest sister. She's also the president of Dreamweavers."

"And what dreams do you weave, Lisa Sinclair?" Pete asked softly.

Everything he said was seductive, Lisa mused, her mouth suddenly going dry. Did he do it deliberately?

She gave herself a silent reminder: of course he did it deliberately. He was a musician, wasn't he? Seduction was his stock-in-trade. "I organize tours in Europe," she answered with as businesslike a tone as she could manage. "Mainly in the south of France."

"They're arts-oriented," Pete stated, suddenly remembering one of the brochures he'd picked up on the riverboat. "As I recall, you offer things like guided pilgrimages to Arles and Van Gogh's sunflower fields, backstage tours of opera houses and theaters, special organ recitals in the great cathedrals of Europe . . ."

"You really are familiar with our operations," Lisa said, obviously surprised.

"I've looked forward to using your services again after that dinner cruise." Especially, Pete thought, now that he'd reached the point where he could afford such luxuries. He remembered that Dream-weavers had organized a group trip for New Orleans jazz fans to this year's Nice and Antibes festivals, yet he still didn't tell Lisa he would be on the Riviera in a couple of weeks. He was drawn to her, but over the years he'd become a careful man. "Do you cater mainly to some kind of cultural elite?" he asked, trying to get a fix on Lisa Sinclair's social circles on the Riviera, wondering whether she was slumming by visiting a Bourbon Street jazz club. What he really wanted to know was whether the lady was out of his league.

Lisa sensed a challenge in his question. She tossed it right back at him. "What do you mean by the term?"

Pete was taken aback. "What do you mean, what do I mean?"

"Cultural elite. Are you asking whether we do tours only for truly knowledgeable arts enthusiasts? For serious critics who attend gallery openings, ballet galas, or whatever, and then write reviews everybody quotes but nobody really understands? Or are you talking about hard-core intellectual snobs?" Lisa gave Pete a pleasant smile. "I just like to nail down the semantics before I answer questions that clearly are meant to get under my skin the way yours just did."

All at once Pete didn't care whether the lady was out of his league or not. He wanted to play. "Let's say, just for the sake of argument, that I was asking whether your clients are all filthy rich."

"Fair enough," Lisa said, discovering that their verbal sparring was adding fuel to the already burning conflagration inside her. Her cool demeanor belied her feelings. "The answer is no—and no. My clients are not all rich." She grinned. "And the rich aren't always filthy."

Unable to suppress a smile, Pete tried to score one more point. "Well, I'm afraid my knowledge of the Riviera is limited to tabloid headlines about movie stars cavorting at the Cannes Film Festival and decadent nobility hopping in and out of one another's staterooms on their mile-long yachts," he said, carefully watching Lisa's reaction to his provocative comments.

To his surprise, she tipped back her head and laughed, then said, "If you were a cavorting movie star or a decadent aristocrat playing musical staterooms, would you actually pay good money to have Dreamweavers put you on a bus to the classical antiquities museums of Provence?"

Pete laughed with her. "I guess myths die hard," he conceded. "So the Riviera isn't the playground of the privileged after all?"

"Sure it is," Lisa said. "But not exclusively. There are less racy but more realistic images than the ones the tabloids offer, if you'd care to hear them."

"Straight from the lips of one who knows," Pete said, his gaze focused on Lisa's tempting mouth.

Disconcerted by the heat that sizzled through her,

LIsa felt her grin waver a little. She spoke as if by rote. "The Côte d'Azur is as accessible to backpacking students and the average tourist as to the well-heeled visitor," she informed Pete. "There are lots of decent but inexpensive hotels, moderate restaurants, and plenty of activities that don't involve spending a centime. You don't have to thrust out a platinum credit card to stroll along a seaside promenade, and the plane trees lining the sidewalks offer the same shade to everyone."

"There seems to be a streak of fierce loyalty in you," Pete commented, aware of the slight strain behind Lisa's monologue. He hoped he was the cause.

Lisa couldn't meet his steady gaze any longer. Suddenly she became very absorbed in the designs she was drawing on her moisture-beaded glass.

"I noticed you used the term Côte d'Azur, not Riviera," Pete said in an effort to keep the conversation going. He couldn't remember when he'd so enjoyed talking with a woman.

"It's a habit," Lisa answered, forcing herself to face Pete again, refusing to let him know how much he unnerved her. But her pride was her downfall. The eyes looking into hers were uncannily like the clear, cobalt blue of the Mediterranean, and Lisa felt as if she could drown in them.

She swallowed hard and went on automatically, barely aware of what she was saying. "An obscure, late nineteenth-century poet who came from the region of France known as the Côte d'Or—or Gold Coast—was taken enough with the dazzling blue of the sea at the Riviera to write a book called *Côte d'Azur*—the Azure Coast." Throughout her entire speech, Lisa found herself drawn hypnotically into Pete's special azure world. She blinked, as if to shut out a too-brilliant light. "The . . . the poet himself is pretty much forgotten, but his phrase has become part of the language."

"Spoken like a first-rate tour guide," Pete said, unable to resist teasing her.

Realizing how pedantic she must have sounded, Lisa came to her senses and laughed, this time at herself. "I no longer lead the Dreamweavers day trips myself, but I do tend to sound like a human travelogue from time to time," she said, rolling her eyes in mock despair.

Pete grinned. He liked this woman. "Are you in New Orleans because of the packages you've put together for the upcoming jazz festivals in your neck of the woods?" he asked casually.

"Oh, no," Lisa answered. "All those plans have been in place for some time. I'm just here for a regular meeting with Stefanie and the rest of the head office people—and a visit, of course."

"You and Stefanie are close, I gather," Pete remarked, careful not to reveal the twinge of envy he felt for anyone whose family seemed openly affectionate and supportive. "I'd venture to say you're pretty fond of all your sisters."

Lisa cocked her head to one side and shot him a quizzical look. "What makes you say so?"

He gave a little shrug. "It's fairly obvious. If you can work together so successfully in a business that's known for cutthroat competitiveness, there must be a lot of mutual respect and friendship among you."

Lisa took a measured sip of her drink. "Interesting," she murmured as she put down her glass.

"Why?" Pete asked. "Am I wrong?"

She shook her head. "Not at all. We do have a

close family, including our parents, though half the time I'm not even sure where Mom and Dad are, but—"

"Why wouldn't you know where your parents are?" Pete interrupted, too curious to let Lisa's throwaway remark go by.

"My folks are involved in anthropological studies," Lisa explained, smiling as she realized how strange her comment must have sounded to someone who didn't know anything about her background. "Their work takes them to a lot of remote spots of the world. Sometimes the communications systems literally consist of drumbeats and smoke signals."

Pete decided to file away the string of questions that particular tidbit of information inspired. With any luck, he would get a chance to ask them later. "Okay, let's get back to why you found it interesting that I guessed at the closeness among the Dreamweavers sisters."

"Oh, it's just that some people seem to assume that because we all live so far apart, and appear to be quite different from one another, we're emotionally distanced as well. A couple of gossipy travel writers have hinted that there's a seething rivalry among us. There isn't. How about you?" she asked brightly, tired of having the spotlight beamed on herself. "Are you part of a big, happy family? Lots of music and laughter? Everyone bursting with pride over your success?"

Pete frowned. He picked up his glass for the first time and downed a healthy slug of bourbon. "No," he said quietly, leaving his answer at that, the abrupt word hanging over them like a cloud.

Lisa wasn't sure what to say next. Pete's clipped response didn't encourage any more questions.

At that moment, a chance look at the redhead still perched on a stool at the piano bar startled Lisa; she found herself pinioned by a hostile stare. Lisa barely controlled a shudder. She wasn't sure whether or not the redhead had a claim on Pete, but jealous scenes over a man weren't her cup of tea.

She glanced at her watch, wondering when Pete's break would be over.

Sensing Lisa's tension, Pete assumed his abruptness about his family had caused it. But what more could he have said? He wasn't from a big family, or a demonstratively happy one. His love of music had been endured not encouraged. When he'd been growing up, there hadn't been a lot of laughter in the Cochrane household. As far as he could tell, he hadn't made anybody back home especially proud.

When he noticed Lisa peeking at her watch again, Pete decided he'd made a mistake. Why was he trying to get to know this woman? Sure, there was some kind of strange chemistry between them, but she was making it pretty clear she didn't want to follow up on it. Neither did he, for that matter. And how did he know she wasn't seeing someone in France? Probably some titled, continental type.

Something in Pete rebelled at that thought. Lisa Sinclair didn't strike him as a woman who would be involved with one man and look at another the way she'd looked at him.

An idea struck him. Not a very novel one, but a logical one: Why didn't he just come right out and ask?

He wasn't sure. And he didn't like the feeling of being so nonplussed around a woman, so off center. Maybe, he thought, his sophisticated lady was much too sophisticated for him.

He decided to go for broke. "Lisa, I think you're as bowled over by what's been building between us this evening as I am," he said, his gaze holding hers. "Why are you pretending you're not?"

Lisa stared at him, caught completely off guard. She'd grown up with people who had a habit of being brutally honest, but she wasn't used to encountering it outside her family. "I'm not pretending," she answered, deciding that such a direct question rated a truthful response. "I'm resisting. I don't want anything to build between us."

Pete hadn't expected such a straight answer. In a strange way, it pleased him. But he wanted to know why Lisa was resisting an attraction she wasn't trying to deny. Were piano players off-limits in her circles? Did she feel she was too cosmopolitan for an untitled American? Or *was* there someone else? "What's the problem?" he asked with a forced smile. "Are you taken?"

Lisa hesitated. Honesty was one thing, but she owed Pete Cochrane no explanations. And perhaps she'd better get serious about keeping him at arm's length. "What an odd thing to ask," she said. "Am I taken? You make me sound like a seat in a theater."

Suddenly Pete felt like an idiot—especially since he had to admit that Lisa was right. "I guess I did use an unfortunate turn of phrase," he said with a sheepish smile. "Sorry."

Lisa groaned inwardly. Why had he reacted that way? He should have responded to her snippy comment with a nasty comeback, not an apology. "I'm the one who's sorry," she said with a sigh. "And to answer the question you meant to ask: No, I'm not involved with anyone else. I'm resisting this attraction for other reasons, one of them simply being the airliner for France I'm boarding in the morning." Abruptly deciding a change of subject was in order, she asked, "Are you planning another album soon?"

"Should I plan one?" Pete said, bemused by Lisa's total lack of guile. He'd never met a woman quite like her.

Lisa relaxed a little, comfortable with the subject of Pete's music. "Well, I listen constantly to the one I have, and I'd love to hear more of your work, if that means anything."

Pete's too-vivid imagination conjured up several provocative settings in which Lisa might listen to his music. "It means a great deal," he said, surprised to discover that he meant it.

His voice was a caress that threatened to make Lisa want to forget why she should resist him. But she told herself she'd better make the effort to remember. "Have you been doing any composing?" she asked. "Your interpretations of the old standards are wonderful, but I really like your original numbers. 'Manhattan Concerto' is the best thing I've heard in years. It's so . . . lush."

Pete burst out laughing, partly from unexpected delight, partly from another bout of self-consciousness. "You have no mercy," he teased. "You claim you don't want anything to build between us, yet everything you say and do is geared to make me more besotted with you. You actually own my album and call my 'Manhattan Concerto' the best thing you've heard in years, and you expect me to stay cool? Have a heart, woman!"

Lisa couldn't help laughing with him, certain he was exaggerating his feelings. "What do you want me to do? Say I *don't* like the concerto? Melt down the album?"

"I have a thought, Lisa. Stick around for my next set. I'll do some numbers I've been working on, and you can give me your opinion."

"You're joking," Lisa said, though she wasn't sure he was. "I don't know what sells albums."

"You know as much as anyone and more than most." It occurred to Pete that he was being a bit presumptuous. Maybe she didn't want to stay. But he couldn't help coaxing her. "I don't pay well," he said with a grin, "but I have enough pull with the bartender to get an extra bowl of salted almonds for your table."

Lisa shook her head and laughed again. "How can I refuse?"

Pete's rush of pleasure startled him. He couldn't understand why it was so important to have Lisa stay through the set, to get a chance to sit with her again during the next break. But he couldn't deny how much it mattered.

If he could keep her from leaving until he'd finished for the night, he thought, he might be able to talk her into having a cup of coffee with him. Maybe he could find out why she was so standoffish. There was even a chance she'd stop *being* so standoffish. "Time to earn my keep," he said, getting to his feet. "I have to play a request first. Then I'll do some experimental pieces." Quickly he returned to the piano, as if he had to get there and start weaving musical magic before Lisa changed her mind and left.

Despite her determination not to be drawn into his alluring web, Lisa was elated by the heady excitement Pete had generated just by being with her for a few minutes. And when he sat down at the piano, grinned, and winked at her, she felt her heart turn over.

The redhead spoke to him. With a nod, he began playing "Georgia." The woman blew him a kiss, then turned to shoot Lisa a look of triumph.

Instantly Lisa regretted her promise to stay. She wanted to leave, to forget she'd met Pete Cochrane, to eradicate from her memory his flirtatious words, his ridiculously blue eyes, his winning smile. Hadn't she learned her lesson all those months ago?

Because she'd made him a promise, she listened to most of his set, then took a pen and notepad from her bag, wrote a few lines in her neat, careful hand, and motioned to the waiter. "Could you give this note to Mr. Cochrane?" She pressed a bill into the man's hand and smiled brightly. "Deliver it *after* I leave, please." When he nodded and thanked her for the generous tip, she stood up. "I'm on my way, gang. I have an early plane to catch, and I'd like one last gossip session with Steffie before bedtime."

Justin leapt to his feet. "I'll get you a taxi."

"I can manage," Lisa protested.

Roberta spoke up. "Actually, I was just thinking that we should go too. It's getting awfully late."

Lisa shook her head. "But I don't want to spoil your evening. . . ."

"You're not spoiling anyone's evening," Roberta said firmly, then smiled with feminine understanding. "Except perhaps Pete Cochrane's. And maybe you're making a wise decision. He's the kind of man a woman could fall hard for. And you don't want to fall, right?"

Justin gave a rude snort that eloquently expressed his opinion of the whole situation. Otherwise, he said nothing except to bid good night to the members of their group who were staying.

Lisa waved to Harry Milton as she passed him, and to a few other people she recognized in the crowd, but didn't look back at the piano bar until she reached the club's exit. Then, turning briefly, she met Pete's gaze. She was shocked by his expression. He looked hurt—truly, deeply hurt.

Barely managing a smile and a casual little wave to him, she made her escape before she changed her mind. There was nothing to be gained by getting to know a man like Pete Cochrane, she told herself.

And he wasn't really hurt. Even if he was, it was a superficial wound. The redhead or some other Florence Nightingale would kiss it better.

"Coward," Justin muttered. "You know, there's racism and sexism and even ageism. What would we call your particular brand of bigotry, Lisa? That guy really liked you, and you brushed him aside. And why? Just because he's a musician. You're prejudiced against the members of the very profession you admire above all others. I don't get it."

"I'm not prejudiced," Lisa said lightly, battling an urge to go back in and try to erase the wounded expression from Pete's eyes. "I'm just a realist, Justin. Musicians are . . ." She smiled. "How can I say this nicely? Most of them are committed to a lifestyle that isn't conducive to building honest relationships. How's that?"

"As bafflegab goes, it's not bad," Justin answered.

Lisa kept her smile in place. "Let me put it another way, then: Could we please, please, please drop the subject of my love life?"

"Or the lack of one," Justin muttered, making sure he had the last word. A taxi pulled up at his signal, and he opened the car door. "We'll get the next cab," he explained.

Lisa nodded. He and Roberta were heading in a different direction, so it made sense to go separately. "I'll miss you both," she said, hugging each of them.

"We'll miss you, too, squirt," Justin said. "Come back soon."

Blinking back sudden, stinging tears, Lisa smiled. "I will if you two ever set a wedding date."

He grinned. "Maybe when we do, Bobby-Jo and I will hire a certain piano player for our reception."

"You do and I'll renege on my promise to be your best man, Justin Fuller." Lisa climbed into the taxi. "See you at the altar," she said just before Justin closed the door.

Her smile faded as the cab pulled into the heavy late-night traffic of the French Quarter.

Each time she left New Orleans to go back to France, the good-byes got harder. No matter how much she loved the Côte d'Azur, and no matter how many interesting people she knew there, she often felt like a homesick kid at summer camp.

And the worst part of the night was ahead. She still had to say good-bye to T.J. and Stefanie. The visit with them had been much too short. Of course, she had to admit, the visits were always too short, no matter how long she stayed.

Giving herself a mental shake, Lisa sat back and concentrated on the enjoyable weeks ahead. The wealth of summer music festivals in Provence would draw some of the best performers in the world to the Côte d'Azur. She might get to see Harry and Sheila Milton and lots of other friendly faces. Anyone with a grain of sense would envy her.

When she couldn't cheer herself up, she silently admitted that what she really felt rotten about was the way she'd walked out on Pete Cochrane. She knew she should have waited to speak to him again at the end of his set. Justin was right. She was a coward.

But if being a coward kept her from being a fool, she reminded herself, she was prepared to paint a wide saffron stripe right down the middle of her back.

Three

Pete read Lisa's note. *I can't wait to buy the new album*, she'd written. *If the numbers you've played tonight are any indication—especially the second one of this last set—the next Pete Cochrane collection will be even more of a winner than the first. Thanks for making my final night in New Orleans so special. All the best, Lisa. P.S. Thanks for the almonds.*

He couldn't fault the woman's tact. But what else would he expect from such a classy lady?

Still, why she'd gone so abruptly, leaving him with only the note for a souvenir, was beyond him. And why he cared so much was equally perplexing.

He finished the set and got up from the piano.

"How 'bout havin' a drink with Wanda this time, sugar?" the redhead said with a rather challenging smile. "That's my name, by the way."

Pushy types who couldn't take gentle hints deserved to be put off with any handy ploy, Pete told himself, then thought about how uncharacteristically pushy he'd been with Lisa. Maybe he'd deserved what she'd ladled out to him.

He felt only a small twinge of guilt for the lie he was about to tell. "Sorry, miss, my wife doesn't like me to have drinks with other ladies," he said with a forced grin as he headed for Harry Milton's table.

"You're doing some good work," Harry said after Pete had pulled up a chair. "You went a little heavy on the sentimental stuff in the set before last, maybe, but it wasn't hard to see why."

Slightly embarrassed, Pete shrugged. "As the old song says, Harry, it was just one of those things." He tried to stop there, but his curiosity got the best of him. "I gather you know the lady."

Harry took a maddeningly slow sip of his drink before answering. "Sheila and I have met Lisa a few times, mostly at parties, private jam sessions, that kind of scene. And just for the record, Pete, I've watched a lot of guys try a lot harder than you did to make time with her. Nobody gets anywhere. Your interest in her is a healthy sign, though. It shows you've outgrown the Christine types."

"If I were attracted even slightly to another Christine, I'd figure it was time to check into a rubber room," Pete said with a disgusted roll of his eyes. "By the way, Harry, I don't believe I ever did thank you for being my crying towel after that episode. I must have tried your patience."

"You did, but it was understandable. Anyway, I don't want to drop the subject of Lisa Sinclair. She's a special girl."

Pete laughed. "I believe you, Harry. She's very special. She's also gone. And by tomorrow at this time, she'll be in France."

"Where you'll be in a couple of weeks," Harry pointed out.

"If I couldn't sweet-talk the lady tonight, what makes you think I could do it on her home turf? Or that I'd bother to try?"

Harry grinned and shook his head. "I saw you two together. I nearly called the fire department. What's the matter, kid? Are you afraid you can't compete with the crowd Lisa hobnobs with on the Riviera?"

"What crowd is that?" Pete asked.

"Oh, the artsy types, the international set, the millionaires with yachts that look like cruise liners."

"So she *does* move in those circles," Pete murmured.

"I had a suspicion your reverse snobbishness might bubble to the surface," Harry said. "Don't let it. Lisa's no social climber."

Pete was surprised by his friend's adamance. "I didn't suggest she was. I didn't even think it. The woman's successful in her own right. She doesn't have to ride on somebody else's coattails."

All at once, Pete realized why Lisa not only fascinated him but unnerved him a little. Obviously he'd sensed immediately that she wasn't one of the female hangers-on he encountered on the club circuit. He was drawn to her because she was different, but that very difference gave him pause.

The sensible thing would be to forget all about her, he told himself, but she wasn't going to be easy to forget. Those huge eyes with their secret lode of emeralds would stay with him for a long, long time.

Still, a small voice of reason kept telling Pete that Lisa Sinclair didn't figure in his plans. His career presented enough of a struggle, enough stretching to reach goals just beyond his grasp. He certainly didn't need a similar challenge in other areas of his life.

Realizing that Harry was watching him, Pete

laughed and said gruffly, "I seem to be a bit smitten with an unattainable lady, Harry. How did I let such a fool thing happen at this stage of my life?"

The older man shrugged. "It's a lot like getting zapped by lightning. You don't have a whole lot of say in the matter."

With another laugh, Pete got to his feet. He had a few more buddies to say hello to before his break ended. "I'll see you and Sheila in Nice. Thanks for dropping by on one of your rare nights off."

"My pleasure," Harry answered. "By the way, if you're interested in my opinion of your work . . ."

Pete was shocked that he hadn't spent any time drawing on Harry's experience and good taste for some constructive criticism. "I'm always interested, Harry. From you, all suggestions are welcome."

"The second number you played in the last set: what's it called?"

"I haven't come up with a name yet," Pete said, intrigued by the fact that both Lisa and Harry had zeroed in on a composition he was struggling to develop. "In fact, I'm still not sure I'm happy with the thing."

Harry nodded. "Well, work on it, Pete. It has a lot of potential. Really first-rate stuff. But for my money, it was over too soon. I'd have enjoyed hearing you fool around with it a bit more. Don't worry if what you want doesn't happen right away. Be patient. The best things often take time to develop."

Pete grinned. "Are we talking about music or Lisa Sinclair?"

"Maybe both," Harry answered, then raised his glass to Pete. "No, definitely both."

•   •   •

Lisa sat at her desk, her back to the window, the slanted rays of the Mediterranean sun warming the nape of her neck as she bent over her work with the side of her head resting on her hand, her fingers splayed through her hair to hold back a stubborn cowlick.

She finished signing the last of a stack of checks, sat back, and stared at her cluttered desk in amazement. "I'm caught up," she murmured. "At long last, I'm actually caught up."

"And just in time," Colette Deveraux said as she breezed in from the outer office carrying the envelopes she'd just typed. "Listen," she said, cocking her head to one side.

Lisa smiled, as she usually did when Colette was around. The twenty-year-old receptionist was wonderfully Gallic, with her stylishly cropped dark hair, the designer outfits she bought for a song in sample sizes, the appealing French lilt in her voice.

But Lisa had another reason for smiling. "It's the jazz parade," she said, carefully pushing back her spindly-legged antique chair and tossing down her pencil to hurry to the window.

As the pencil rolled across the surface of Lisa's desk and fell off the edge, carrying several papers with it to the carpet, Colette laughed. "Lisa, when are you going to get a proper place to work? This funny little escritoire may have been fine for a lady in a powdered wig writing quill-pen notes to her lover, but I've wanted to ask you for ages: What possessed you to buy it?"

Pushing back the lace curtains and struggling to open the high, narrow window, Lisa said over her shoulder, "I couldn't help myself. The poor thing was so scarred and dusty, and seemed so lonely sitting in that snobbish dealer's shop, as if it knew it didn't belong, I just had to take it."

Colette shook her head and moved to the jammed window to help Lisa open it. "You also had to take the chair, the filing cabinet, the Madame de Pompadour chaise longue—you know, most people drag home stray kittens or puppies, or if they're like your sister Morgan, stray people. I've never met anyone before who can't turn her back on rejected furniture."

When the window finally gave way, Lisa grinned at Colette. "The parade's getting closer. It'll come right by us. Listen to that trumpet!"

"You're like my little brother," Colette teased. "Jean-Paul loves parades almost as much as you do."

Folding her arms on one side of the sill and leaving room beside her for Colette, Lisa leaned out to watch for the approaching procession of festival musicians. "It's like being in New Orleans again," she said with a happy sigh. "Back home, you never know when a marching band will come around some corner and make you want to dance." She smiled as the music came closer. "I don't believe I'd want to live in a place that didn't have parades."

A few minutes later, even Colette couldn't pretend to be blasé; she applauded excitedly when the line of musicians filled the street below. "Let me help you tidy your office so we can go up to Cimiez together," Colette said when the last strains of the parade had faded.

Lisa raised her brows in surprise. "When did you become enough of a jazz lover to want to take in the festival performances?"

As she began stuffing Lisa's checks into their proper envelopes, Colette giggled. "Last night, when I met my adorable drummer from London. He said he'd meet me at the arena today."

Lisa groaned inwardly. Women never learned. "Beware of itinerant troubadours," she said, filing invoices. "They'll make you feel you're the only woman in the world—but you soon find out that you're not."

"I look at things a different way," Colette said. "I make a man feel as if he's the only one in the world." She paused to smile and wink mischievously at Lisa. "But I soon find out that he's not!"

Laughing, Lisa decided not to worry about Colette. In fact, she thought, it might be a good idea to take a few lessons from the girl.

The cadences of modern jazz echoed among ancient ruins as the Cimiez Arena was transformed into an open-air, musical marketplace.

Tiny by the standards of Imperial Rome, the amphitheater that had been built in the time of Augustus Caesar was much the worse for the ravages of centuries, but still had enough charm to offer a perfect setting for a modern-day festival that would have had Nero reaching for his fiddle.

Lisa wandered with Colette from one band to another, smiling at the way a joyous bebop bounced off someone's Cry-Me-A-River blues and over the fact that no one seemed to mind the strange overlap of sounds.

As a tenor sax crooned its sad story, Lisa remembered when the wail of that particular instrument would have twisted her stomach into a knot. But now it didn't bother her at all, and she realized that time had cured her of the proverbial man who got away. She was glad her saxophone player had disappeared into the netherworld of some smoky basement club in Berlin with his pretty fräulein. For the life of her, Lisa couldn't remember why she'd cared at all, or why, in the first place, she'd broken her no-musicians rule for the insensitive, mendacious little . . .

Some cure, she thought, laughing at herself.

But even superficial wounds left scars, she had to admit, and she would do well to remember it. If she'd been foolish enough to follow up on the intense feelings Pete Cochrane had aroused in her, she could have been in the midst of some major healing period by now, instead of just settling for the nagging, inexplicable sense of loss that hit her whenever those cobalt eyes popped up in her memory.

Fortunately, she thought with an ironic sigh, that blip in her emotional controls happened only during most of her waking hours and in no more than half of her dreams.

Pete wasn't surprised when he spotted Lisa in the crowd milling around the arena. After all, he hadn't been able to stop watching for her on every street, in every park, and every shop, almost from the first moment his plane had touched down at the Nice airport. He'd known she'd had to show up sooner or later.

Standing near the area where another jazz pianist was playing—a former teacher of Pete's, in fact, who'd asked him to sit in for a number—Pete had found his gaze following every honey blond in sight. It amazed him how many model-slim women with pale, chin-length hair there were. And it was just as remarkable what a letdown each of them turned out to be.

Until Lisa.

When Pete saw her, he wondered almost guiltily how he could have mistaken any mere facsimile for her, even for a fleeting moment.

Her style was so distinctive, he thought: the silent-screen-heroine hairdo, the sleeveless ivory dress that fell in a straight, narrow line of tailored pleats from Lisa's slim shoulders to just below her knee, giving her the look of Gatsby's Daisy.

Needing a moment to deal with the sudden excitement of seeing Lisa, Pete was glad she hadn't noticed him. She was chatting with a young, dark-haired girl and a drummer named Dave Something. Pete recognized him as a member of a little band from London that produced some very weird sounds they called experimental music. Good-looking in an angular Jeremy Irons way, and sheathed in skintight black leather pants that looked hot and uncomfortable in the July heat, the Englishman had his arm draped around the shoulders of Lisa's companion—and his eyes all over Lisa.

Instinctively Pete wanted to go over and slug the guy. But a brawl over a girl was far down on Pete's scale of cool, so he searched his mind for a better approach.

He moved closer to the piano, where his friend had just ended a number. "I've changed my mind," Pete said. "If you still want me to sit in, I'm game. But no intro, okay? Just let me play one number, and then I'm gone. The Phantom of the Festival."

Lisa's smile for Colette's drummer was as frigid as a winter mistral. She wondered if Colette realized that Dave's fidelity quotient was highly flexible.

As he boasted about his little avant-garde jazz group, Lisa couldn't imagine what Colette found so adorable about the self-centered creep. But the girl seemed so delighted that she'd finally met up with Dave, Lisa decided just to get out of the way and allow Colette to have her festival romance without enduring warning glances from a sadder-but-wiser older woman. The gap between her age and Colette's sometimes seemed to Lisa more like decades than a scant six years. "Will you two excuse me?" she said with a forced smile. "I just spied a friend of mine from—" She swallowed hard as a startling, distinctive sound sent shivers up her spine.

Was she hearing things? Had she listened longingly to Pete Cochrane's album once too often? Had she become so addicted, she was suffering hallucinatory withdrawal symptoms?

She pivoted very slowly as the seductive phrases of "Sophisticated Lady" rekindled the fires inside her. And then her gaze was locked on Pete Cochrane's penetrating cobalt eyes.

After a long, electrically charged moment, he grinned and winked. It took a massive effort from Lisa to keep her knees from buckling.

She was transfixed, barely able to nod, when Colette said something about seeing her later.

Aware that he had Lisa under his musical spell, Pete played each haunting phrase seductively. Lisa responded as though his hands were stroking her body, his mouth grazing her lips, his breath fanning her sensitive skin as he whispered erotically in her ear.

Caught without any of her defenses in place, Lisa was unable to stem the flow of warmth that coursed through her like heated brandy.

Pete was urged on by the subtle, compelling magnetism of Lisa's reaction. He saw the quick rise and fall of her high, gently rounded breasts, watched her lips part, her eyes darken.

"Nice," Pete's former teacher said when the song was over. "Your touch just keeps getting better, kid."

Pete smiled absently, relinquished the keyboard to its rightful owner, and went to Lisa, hearing the applause of the surrounding crowd as if through a fog. "Hi there," he said softly.

She gave him a hesitant smile, shy in the knowledge that he knew how he'd made her feel. The fact that he'd stopped playing hadn't quieted her pulse or quelled the flames inside her. The familiar, spicy male scent of him was as intoxicating as his sensual keyboard harmonies, and as he stood close to her, tall and muscular and utterly gorgeous in casual white slacks and a blue polo shirt, she wasn't sure what was keeping her from swooning into his arms. Even his voice, quietly resonant yet warmed by a soft rasp, had the effect of rich, thick sable drawn slowly over bare skin. "You didn't mention that you were coming to Nice," she murmured.

Pete was pleased by the slight tremor in her voice. "As the recipient of your charming yet decisive note, I think I'm justified in saying that you didn't give me much chance to mention anything," he answered.

"Perhaps I didn't," Lisa said, but conceded only part of his point. "Still, I think there were moments when it would have been . . . well, convenient for you to have told me. I can't help wondering why you didn't."

Pete chuckled. Lisa wasn't going to make anything easy for him. "I can't help wondering the same thing," he admitted, then added, "Maybe we should talk about it." He'd meant to use the lead-in as a ploy to ask Lisa to have dinner with him, but he didn't get the chance. Instead, he found himself buttonholed at that moment by a young man sporting the pale skin, long ponytail, and black turtleneck of the typical fine arts student.

"Pete Cochrane," the student said, then went on in fractured English. "You are Pete Cochrane, *oui?* I 'ave never seen the . . . the photograph. I did not . . . how do you say, recon . . . recognize you. But I know your music, *m'sieur.* I am a pianist *aussi.*" He thrust a pencil and notepad at Pete. "I will be so 'appy if you will give your autograph, *s'il vous plaît?*"

Trying to shift his train of thought from Lisa to this unexpected fan, Pete just stared for a moment.

"I did tell you that you were a big hit here, remember?" Lisa said.

Pete smiled quizzically, surprised as well as uncomfortable with this kind of attention. But fans weren't to be taken lightly. Accepting the pencil and pad, he signed his name, at the same time chatting in French about the boy's studies and the various festivals he'd taken prizes in.

Lisa stared at Pete. His command of the language was perfect.

When the student had left, Pete turned again to Lisa, wondering how he could pick up the thread of the conversation and follow it back to the point where he'd been about to ask her out to dinner.

"My goodness, I feel silly," Lisa said, trying to look balefully at Pete despite her grin.

"Why?" Pete asked.

"Côte d'Or? Côte d'Azur?" Lisa said, batting her lashes as she reminded him of the long-winded tour-guide number she'd done back in New Orleans, complete with translations.

Pete laughed. Lisa's manner was the closest thing to a coquettish simper he'd heard since a flower girl in a French nightclub had tried to sell him violets. "Right," he said, finally realizing what she meant. "I should have told you then that I spoke French, but—"

"No, Pete, I shouldn't have assumed you couldn't," Lisa interrupted. "Especially since the notes on the back of your album cover mentioned that you'd launched your career with an apprenticeship in *le jazz hot* in Paris. It's just that lots of musicians play Paris clubs; not too many learn the language."

"I didn't learn French as a musician," Pete explained. "I studied languages in college—to prepare myself for the career I'd expected to have in the diplomatic corps. Somehow, in Paris, everything changed."

Lisa smiled, but Pete's comment brought her back to reality with a thud. "In Paris, all the rules are different," she said, quoting what her saxophone player had told her in a Left Bank club as he'd packed his gear for his gig in West Germany—and packed her pride and naive trust along with it.

She searched her mind for a graceful exit line. Her attraction to Pete Cochrane was too compelling. She had to resist it.

Sensing a sudden change in Lisa, Pete wondered if Harry Milton had been wrong about no one getting anywhere with her. The shadow that had crossed her eyes at the mention of Paris seemed to suggest otherwise. She was closing down, Pete thought with a ripple of panic. After the way she'd opened to him, surrendering to his music just as she had in New Orleans, she was retreating again. She was getting ready to bolt—a repeat of what had happened in New Orleans.

Pete didn't want to let it happen. Not this time. "Lisa—"

Once again, he was interrupted. For a person who was something of a loner, he thought disgustedly, he'd become awfully popular all of a sudden.

"Sorry if I'm interrupting anything, but you gotta come with me, Pete," Tony Miller, his agent said. "You've been looking for a synthesizer man to work with you on the arrangements for your album, and I think I've found him. He's playing now, over on the far side of the grounds. But he's almost through his set, so we gotta move. I want you to hear this guy."

Though there was no way Pete could refuse, he didn't want to lose his second chance with Lisa. He turned to ask her to go with him to hear the musician, but it was her turn to be distracted, a small gaggle of tourists claiming her attention. "Lisa, let's catch up with each other later," Pete said as Tony kept urging him along.

With a noncommittal nod, Lisa forced herself to smile politely at the retired American schoolteachers who were, she was glad to hear, raving about the Dreamweavers bus excursion to Marseilles, Avignon, and Aix-en-Provence they'd taken a few days earlier. "It went like clockwork," one of the ladies said. "You people have everything down to a science. And that tour guide—she should be a teacher herself."

"Marie is wonderful," Lisa said, her gaze darting toward Pete every few seconds until he was out of sight. "She's our senior guide."

"Well, we're going to spread the word," a plump, motherly woman said. "We'll recommend Dreamweavers to any of our friends who are planning vacations—and we mean we'll promote all your company's branches. I've never been so impressed, Miss Sinclair. You should be very proud."

Lisa gave the woman a smile that was genuine in its warmth, despite her temporary distraction. It always pleased her to hear good things about Dream-weavers.

She chatted for a few more minutes with the little group, then moved around the arena, enjoying brief visits with musicians she'd met over the years as well as some of the New Orleans jazz fans who'd come to Nice on the Dreamweavers festival tour.

At one point, she found herself within a few feet of Pete. His back was to her, but she could overhear his conversation with the same earnest young man he'd talked to earlier.

"I am a very serious student, *m'sieur*," the boy was saying in French, obviously working up his courage for something that was important to him. "I know you are here on vacation, but if I could have just one lesson with you, one hour, it would mean so much to me. I am preparing for an important audition, so . . ." He hesitated, then thrust out his chin and asked, "What is your charge, please?"

Lisa wondered how Pete would put off the boy gracefully.

But she was more surprised by Pete's response than she'd been when she'd discovered he could speak French. "I'll give you a lesson every morning except on the weekend, if you wish," he told the boy after a moment's thought.

"But I doubt that I could afford so many sessions," the student protested with a look that suggested he was considering selling his grandmother if he thought he could raise the money that way.

"You can afford them," Pete said. "All I charge is what some of the old pros charged me when I was at your stage of the game: pass it on. Sooner than you can imagine, you'll have a chance to give some new-comer a hand." He chuckled. "I guess in this case it's two hands."

As the boy laughed, Lisa moved away. How easy it was to dwell on the bad instead of the good in peo-ple, she thought, remembering how many examples she'd seen over the years of the easy camaraderie among musicians, the mutual respect, the genuine pleasure they took in helping to hone young talent.

No wonder she liked the breed, she thought. Mu-sicians were pretty decent, harem mentalities and unsettled life-styles notwithstanding.

But for the next hour—until she decided she'd had enough jazz for one night—she carefully avoided Pete Cochrane. Because more than ever, she knew that to get involved with him would lead to a good-bye that would make "The Saxophone Blues" seem like "Happy Days Are Here Again" by comparison.

Four

A soft breeze ruffled the lace curtains in Lisa's office, tickled through her hair, then whispered over her desk to lift a few papers and drop them onto the floor, sending them skittering under the adjacent computer table.

The aggravation of losing her work sheets—thanks to her ridiculously inadequate desk—made Lisa stop long enough to check her watch. To her surprise, it was after eight. She sighed, deciding she'd buried herself in her work as long as she could. It was time to face the night.

She didn't know what to do. She certainly didn't want to go to Cimiez; Pete Cochrane would be there. And the thought of heading home didn't appeal to her: Pete's presence filled even her apartment. Hiding his album behind the others in the record rack hadn't squelched her constant temptation to listen to it.

Dinner at her favorite café and a walk along the Promenade des Anglais seemed like a reasonably safe idea, she decided as she knelt to pick up the papers.

On her hands and knees, she crawled around the desk, then under it and the computer table, gathering up the papers on which she'd roughed out several new tour ideas, complete with cost projections, potential revenue, and promotional schemes. With a touch of amusement as she bumped her head on the desk and swore softly, she wondered what her sisters would think of their prim-and-proper, ultra-efficient sibling if they could see her now.

Absentmindedly humming as she retrieved the scattered sheets, Lisa scurried between the legs of her desk to sort and stack the papers, totally oblivious that she was doing a perfect vocalization of the Cochrane jazz riffs she'd heard so often.

Suddenly she noticed the toes of a pair of gray leather loafers in her doorway. Just above the shoes were two perfectly creased gray linen pant legs. Above those was the lower half of a summer-weight, black and white silk tweed blazer. Her visitor, Lisa mused, was a dapper fellow. Probably he was looking for the tailor, whose offices and workrooms were one floor up.

She poked her head out from under the desk, still absently shooby-dooing. Her gaze moved slowly upward as her intuition went into overdrive. "Shooby-doo . . . wah," she whispered in a lame finish to the song as her eyes confirmed the warning of her crazed pulse.

Pete Cochrane hunkered down, quietly applauding. "And shooby-doo-wah to you, Miss Sinclair. I couldn't have played it better myself. What are you doing down there? Or should I say, doo-wahing down there?

Is this one of those new, experimental management techniques, or are you expecting an earthquake?"

To Lisa's horror, she felt her cheeks turn flame red. Lisa Sinclair, blushing? Impossible. Was there no *end* to the different ways this man affected her? "I—I—My desk is too small. The top of it, I mean."

Pete nodded as if he understood perfectly. "So you decided to try working under it?"

"No, no. I dropped all these papers because . . ." Suddenly the humor of the scene hit Lisa, and she burst out laughing. "Of all the people to find me like this, why did it have to be you?"

Pete felt a glow of pleasure race through him at Lisa's unconscious admission that he was special to her. He was glad he'd given in to the maddening impulse to seek her out when he hadn't run into her again at the festival grounds, and hadn't found her at the piano bar where Harry Milton had said she might go. He'd considered the possibility that she was avoiding him. But she'd gotten under his skin, and despite his own reservations about getting involved with any woman, he'd swallowed his pride enough to make one more try.

She was so lovely, he thought, reeling from the sheer pleasure of seeing her again. Even crawling around under a desk she was the essence of elegance, of graceful, stylish femininity, in a pleated white skirt and a spring green shell top that was reflected in the secret jewels of her eyes. His sophisticated lady, he thought with a strange rush of tenderness. There she was, peering up at him like an impish waif caught doing something she shouldn't. "Do you plan to stay under there?" he asked, his voice husky. "If you do, may I join you?"

"I'll come out," Lisa said, wondering how much

Pete had seen and heard of her undignified performance of the past few minutes.

Curling his fingers around her upper arms, he helped her to her feet. It was the gesture of a perfect gentleman, Lisa thought, except that he didn't let go. He just kept looking down at her, gazing into her eyes until she was glad he was still supporting her; there wasn't much chance her legs would do the job. "Hello," she said softly, her eyes not leaving his even as she carefully placed the gathered papers on her desk.

Pete's fingers tightened around her slender arms. He knew he should release her, but he couldn't. For one thing, he felt dizzy. Her eyes were giving him vertigo. And they took his breath away.

It occurred to Lisa that there was a question she ought to be asking Pete. After several moments she finally thought of it. "What are you doing here?"

"You've disappeared on me twice," he said quietly. "I decided to find out why." He drew Lisa still closer to him, and noticed that she didn't pull away.

Lisa blinked slowly, not sure that what was happening was real. "How did you find me?"

"I called you at home and there was no answer. Just on the off chance you might be working late, I looked up your office address, strolled by, saw a light on, and . . ." Pete gazed down at Lisa's parted lips and forgot what he was saying. Breathing deeply, drinking in the elusive scent of her perfume, a subtle blend of musk and exotic flowers that had wafted through his memory at random moments ever since they'd met in New Orleans, he felt his pulse start to race like a teenager's souped-up Chevy careening out of control.

The silence was charged with explosive currents

of suppressed excitement that deeply disturbed Lisa. She told herself she had to defuse the moment. She mustn't give in to the powerful feelings Pete was stirring in her. Flattening her hands on his chest, she meant to push him gently away.

But her resolve was no match for her desire as she felt the wild hammering of Pete's heart and saw the sudden purpose in his mesmerizing blue eyes. And when he brushed his mouth over hers in a tentative caress, she was so disarmed, she simply melted against him.

"Lisa," Pete murmured as he raised his head and looked down at her, startled by the powerful feelings suddenly dominating him, moved by the soft surrender of her response. "Lisa, your kisses do strange things to me."

She laughed shakily. "My kisses? Have I kissed you before now?"

"Haven't you?" Pete said with a tender smile, his eyes searching hers.

Lisa gazed at him for a long moment, then sighed as she twined her arms around his neck. "Oh, yes, Pete," she answered at last. "Many, many times."

He captured her mouth again, this time more boldly, toying with her lips, nipping at them until they were slightly swollen, then soothing them with his tongue.

But suddenly the love play wasn't enough. Pete was gripped by an unexpected, unprecedented need. Cupping one hand behind Lisa's head, he laced his fingers through her hair, his kiss deepening into an urgent demand.

Lisa was consumed by an excitement she'd never known before, so overwhelming it was like being swept up by a tornado, whirled in its wild maelstrom and carried off to an over-the-rainbow realm of sensuality, a magical Oz of pleasure. As her lips parted against his, Pete's tongue made forays into her mouth, creating an instant addiction in Lisa to the sweet, hot taste of him.

The intimacy of the kiss stripped away Lisa's inhibitions as Pete laid bare a need she'd been refusing to acknowledge, a passion he had stirred in her that night in the New Orleans club—or perhaps before then, possibly even as far back as the first time she'd heard his sensitive, strong fingers caressing the piano keys the way they were meant to be caressed, the way a woman was meant to be caressed.

At last he raised his head and looked down at her, his eyes clouded with some emotion Lisa couldn't read.

He managed a smile, but there was a thick hoarseness to his voice as he spoke. "I hadn't intended for things to get so out of control."

Lisa lowered her eyelids, her senses returning enough to allow shock to set in. "I don't know how it happened," she murmured, then stiffened as she realized what Pete must think of her. She wasn't sure what to think of herself. No mindless groupie could have behaved with more abandon.

Aching to tell Pete she wasn't in the habit of surrendering the way she had to him, Lisa nevertheless remained silent, refusing to compound her foolishness by trying to explain it. Pete would think what he would think, she told herself. Nothing she said would make any difference. "Perhaps you should let me go," she suggested.

"There's no perhaps about it," Pete said, still stunned by the impact of the kiss. "If I don't, I'm liable to forget I'm supposed to be at least something of a gentleman." He shook his head and laughed softly. "The trouble is, I'm not certain I *can* let you go. I'm a little shaken up, Lisa."

She smiled, grateful for his tact. From what she could tell, Pete was fully in control of himself, although undeniably aroused. She, on the other hand, felt as if she might shatter into a million pieces right before his eyes. She was certain he knew exactly what effect he'd had on her. It was good of him, she thought, to pretend he was the one on the verge of falling apart.

Pete took a deep breath, held it for a few seconds, then let it out slowly. "Okay. Here goes," he said, trying to sound playful. He removed his arms from around her and drew away as carefully as if she were the topmost ace he'd just placed on a fragile house of cards.

With a shaky laugh, Lisa pushed her fingers through her hair and took a backward step.

It struck her that she'd drifted a long way out of character. Why was she being so passive, waiting for the next turn of events instead of determining it herself? She prided herself on her adeptness at fielding passes, at controlling situations like this one, at handling awkward moments when men wanted more from her than she was willing to give. Why was she suddenly feeling so helpless?

She knew exactly why. This situation was no "pass" to be "handled." She didn't want to harness events and shape them as usual. And she was willing to give Pete everything he asked for and more.

Only after several long, thoughtful moments did Pete speak, his voice so grave and determined it surprised even him. "Okay, Lisa. I've let you go for now, but you won't go very far. Not this time. You've slipped away from me twice. I tried to tell myself it didn't matter. It did matter; does matter. I've been fighting my feelings for you since you walked into that New Orleans club. It's a losing battle, Lisa. And the kiss you and I just shared tells me . . ." He stopped for a moment, as if checking whether it really was Pete Cochrane talking—laid-back, detached, leave-'em-but-don't-love-'em Pete Cochrane. It was. "Let's just say we have a few things to talk about," he added. "Over dinner, for starters."

Excitement and apprehension rippled through Lisa in countless tiny shock waves. She felt panic setting in as Pete's words tumbled through her mind, both reassuring and terrifying her. He did seem to understand that the way she'd reacted to him was special, that she wasn't in the habit of kissing men the way she'd kissed him.

But he now knew for certain that she had no defenses against him. If he chose to press his advantage . . . "I'd better file these things," she said, glancing at the sheaf of papers on her desk. It would give her something to do while she sorted out her emotions.

As she picked them up and took them to the aged, scarred filing cabinet, she tried to make light of the entire situation. "Pete, I'm no one to talk, but you do seem to be a trifle . . . impulsive," she said in a strained voice.

"Perhaps," Pete conceded. *Impulsive* wasn't the word, he thought as he watched Lisa's graceful movements. The truth was, he'd been feeling slightly crazy since he'd first seen this woman. He never had gotten back on track properly.

The drawer of the cabinet stuck when Lisa tugged on it. She gave it a few pulls, then a couple of jiggles, finally a good swat. It jarred loose, and she opened it, then began carefully inserting the papers into their proper files.

"Odd," Pete said with a chuckle, distracted from his troubled thoughts by the incongruity of the lovely Lisa battling with a file drawer. "I'd pictured you in some sleek, high-tech environment."

"So had I, once upon a time," Lisa said, though for the first time since she'd bought her ridiculous office furniture she appreciated its stubborn habits. She had vented some of her inner turmoil by sparring with the file cabinet. She battled with the drawer again before she could get it completely shut, then took a deep breath and turned to face Pete, still at a loss for words.

"I've never seen lace curtains in an office before," Pete remarked as he glanced around the small room. Though he was bemused by Lisa's offbeat office, he mentioned it mainly in an effort to ease the tension. "Or flowered wallpaper," he added.

"I haven't either," Lisa said, returning to her desk to fight with another drawer for possession of her purse. Then she managed a nervous smile. "But once the rest of these rickety antiques were in place, vertical blinds and institutional beige wouldn't have worked."

Pete's curiosity was piqued. "Did the suite come furnished? Is there a lease that doesn't allow any changes, the kind you deal with in a heritage building?"

Lisa laughed and shook her head. "I have to take full responsibility for everything." She smiled fondly at her pitiful excuse for a desk. "Well, not the scratches and gouges in the furniture. I think those happened about fifty years ago. But I bought it all. I wasn't drugged, drunk, or lied to. I knew what I was getting, and I took it anyway."

"Why?" Pete asked, with a grin.

"It's a long story. I don't think I know you well enough to go into it." Purse in hand at last, Lisa dug out her keys and moved from behind her desk. "What it amounts to," she said, taking a white blazer from a small closet and shrugging into it, "is that I seem to have a fatal character flaw that hits me when I go furniture shopping." She looped the gold chain of her white, quilted leather Chanel handbag over her shoulder and smiled brightly at Pete.

"I can't wait until the day you feel you can confide the sorry details," he said as he stepped aside to let Lisa pass through the doorway. It occurred to Pete that she wasn't arguing about going with him for dinner. Her lack of resistance pleased him, but he didn't quite count on it yet.

They picked their way down a narrow, curved staircase with a black wrought-iron banister until they'd reached the ground floor. Pete felt as if he'd stepped back a century or so; like Lisa's own office and her furniture, the building was charming, but it didn't fit the image he'd formed of Dreamweavers, Inc. "I still can't shake my preconceived ideas about you," he said to Lisa as they reached ground level and stepped outside the pale peach, white-trimmed building. "My mental picture had you ensconced in lavish, supermodern corporate digs, not a converted mansion that looks as if it once belonged to the mistress of some nineteenth-century tycoon."

"I'd rather pay high salaries for top staff than cough up unnecessarily steep rent money," Lisa explained absently, her mind still engaged in a debate about whether to make some phony excuse to get out of spending an evening with Pete before it was too late, or throw caution to the winds and accept his tempting dinner invitation. "Besides, I prefer the atmosphere of a place that's been lived in, that has its own history," she said. Then, deciding she sounded rather stuffy, she added, "And I hate places where you can't open the windows."

Pete smiled, studying her. "Come to think of it, my mental picture was off the mark. You don't belong in one of those impersonal buildings with severe lines and mechanically recycled air and walls made of sealed glass. You belong in a place that has a special charm of its own—just like this one." He hesitated, then forged ahead. "Where would you like to have dinner?"

With her mind finally made up to refuse, Lisa was ready with one of the graceful demurrals that had become second nature to her.

But just as she was about to parrot the correct words, she made the mistake of looking into Pete's blue eyes. She was lost. Even if she could disappoint herself by refusing his invitation—and she wasn't sure she was up to that kind of self-denial—she couldn't bear to cause even a hint of the hurt expression she'd seen that night in New Orleans when she'd run out on him. "Any place is fine with me," she said.

Pete's heart went crazy. He'd been prepared to do some persuading; suddenly it wasn't necessary, and he felt like hauling Lisa into his arms out of sheer exuberance. "How about the Chantecler?" he suggested, prepared to splurge.

"The Chantecler is lovely," Lisa answered carefully, wondering if Pete really wanted to go to the luxury dining room of the Hotel Negresco, or just felt he had to demonstrate that he could afford any spot she might choose. Most of the musicians she'd known tended to live for the moment and pay the piper later.

Musicians, she thought, abruptly reminded that Pete was a bona-fide member of the breed she'd declared off-limits. She'd forgotten that vital detail for a little while.

She realized she was going to have to keep a close guard on her feelings. A pleasant little dinner with Pete would have to be the end of it. When it was over, she would allow herself no excuses, no back-tracking. And she wanted no expensive evening to make her feel guilty. "To be honest, Pete, I'd prefer something more homey and down-to-earth than the Chantecler," she told him. "I do have a favorite spot, if you don't mind a suggestion. The atmosphere isn't fancy, but it's pleasant—all old, dark wood and white plaster, chintz curtains, soup served in heavy white tureens, the walls decorated with oil paintings that are anything but old masters yet seem perfect for the surroundings. And the food is terrific, I promise."

Pete would have followed her anywhere. He only hoped Lisa was choosing a simpler restaurant out of real preference, not because she was worried about his pocketbook—or worse, because she didn't want to run into any of her barons or counts or millionaires.

He gave a mental shrug to knock an old chip off his shoulder, then smiled. "Lead on," he said with a slight bow and a courtly sweep of his hand. "Some-one who has to travel as much as I do soon learns to follow the advice of the local townsfolk."

Although Lisa returned his smile, Pete's comment served as another reminder of why she couldn't allow a musician into her life as anything more than a casual acquaintance. It was no accident that they'd been called wandering minstrels since at least the Middle Ages. And wanderers constantly said good-bye. There were enough good-byes in her life already. She didn't need any more.

Lisa recommended the Boeuf Daube Provençal that was her favorite of the restaurant's specialties, and suggested that a carafe of red house wine was perfect to go with the rich beef stew.

Though Pete wondered again if she was being overly considerate of his pocketbook, he went along with her choice—and was glad he had when the food and wine turned out to be superb. "I get a kick out of French waiters," he remarked at the end of the meal.

"You get a kick out of them?" Lisa asked. "Haughty French waiters have been a pet peeve of most visitors to this country for generations."

Pete laughed. "And with good reason, in some cases. But what I enjoy is the way they seem to know instinctively when they're dealing with a Yank. Tonight, for instance, our Gaston spoke to me in English before I'd said a word. Granted, he knows you and is aware you're American. But couldn't I be French? Or is there something about the way I'm dressed? The way I move?"

"Possibly," Lisa said, then added with a teasing grin, "Or Gaston could have made a wild guess after overhearing us speaking English to each other when we walked in."

Pete enjoyed the way the green sparkles in Lisa's huge, lovely eyes so often glinted with humor.

Without those priceless gems, she still would be beautiful, but with them, she was endlessly fascinating.

Another wave of desire swept over him. He couldn't remember ever being so affected by a woman. He searched for something to say, some bit of conversation that might keep him from losing control and leaning across the small table to feast again on Lisa's sweet mouth. But no words came to him, no polite small talk.

As Lisa saw the darkening of Pete's eyes, she felt a flare of familiar heat inside her, a flame that only he seemed capable of igniting. He reached across the table to take one of her hands between his palms, and Lisa found herself thinking again about the pleasures his strong, capable, sensitive hands could offer.

Managing to drag her attention from Pete's hands, she found herself perusing his wide shoulders, his broad chest. She couldn't stop imagining the muscles of his athletic body, remembering vividly the power of his arms, the tautness of his thighs, the heady demands of his mouth.

Exhilarated by what he knew was happening to Lisa as well as to himself, Pete chose not to think about her underlying wariness. He focused instead on the sizzling, mind-numbing heat of her response to his kiss, the suggestion of surrender in her gaze.

He realized that he'd decided to pursue Lisa with the single-mindedness he'd brought to bear throughout his life on anything really important to him. There wasn't much he'd wanted that he hadn't managed to get, and he wanted Lisa Sinclair—and knew she wanted him.

He felt good. Strong. In control. "How about an

after-dinner drink?" he suggested when the coffee had arrived. "Cognac, perhaps? Grand Marnier?"

"Just coffee for me, thank you," Lisa said. The last thing she needed was the erotic warmth of brandy spreading slowly through her body.

Pete turned to their waiter. "I believe I'll have something, Gaston, but I'm not sure what. Is there a local liqueur I should sample?"

Gaston thought for a moment, then gave Pete a bland smile that belied a mischievous twinkle in his dark eyes. "There is a local drink called marc, made from the last pressing of the grapes. But, *m'sieur*, I am not sure you would like it."

"Everything's worth at least one try," Pete said confidently, glancing at Lisa to drive home the double meaning.

"Pete," Lisa said with a hesitant smile. "Gaston's right. You might not like it. That last pressing of the grapes involves the skins and stems. . . ."

"I'll have some," Pete said firmly. He'd followed Lisa's lead since they'd arrived at the restaurant. The restaurant itself had been her choice. Perhaps it was time he asserted himself a little. "When in Nice, do what the Niçoises do," he stated, as if it were a welcome duty.

"Whatever you say," Lisa answered with a shrug and a you-asked-for-it inflection.

When Gaston brought the liqueur, Pete sensed trouble from the way the man stood back to watch him taste it.

Then there was the upward tilt to the corners of Lisa's mouth despite her efforts to suppress her grin. And a glimmer of devilish humor lurked behind her long, dark lashes. That hidden mischief made her all the more intriguing to Pete.

He took a tentative sniff of the drink and knew he'd made a very bad mistake. But he wasn't about to retreat at this point, so he raised the liqueur glass to his lips and tossed back half its contents.

He tried to fake it. Turning to smile at Gaston, he said, "Interesting."

The waiter nodded. "Will there be anything else, *m'sieur?*"

"No, that'll be fine, thank you," Pete answered, his voice strained. "Just the check, please."

With a slight bow and a wicked smile, Gaston moved away.

"How do you like it?" Lisa asked, her lower lip actually quivering with suppressed laughter.

"Great," Pete said. "Just great. Bracing. A real man's drink." Then, giving his head a shake as if to clear it, he added, "If you like lighter fluid, that is." He let out a quiet groan, deciding there was no sense pretending. "It's awful, Lisa. Do I have to drink it? Will I insult Gaston if I don't?"

Lisa leaned forward and spoke confidentially. "If you'll look behind you, you'll see a potted plant. I believe it thrives on that particular drink. Yours wouldn't be the first glass that was tipped into its soil."

Surreptitiously Pete took her advice, then chuckled. "That's what I get for trying to earn my spurs as a local."

Lisa giggled, shaking her head. "I'm sorry for laughing." she told him.

"Your friendly neighborhood waiter is quite the comedian," Pete said, a little embarrassed. He could almost hear his father's favorite "Pride Goeth" homily.

On the other hand, Pete thought as he watched Lisa's eyes continue to sparkle with fun, the unpleasant taste in his mouth was a small payment for the loosening of tension between them. "I'd be willing to bet that Gaston's white lightning is made especially for gullible tourists," Pete added, deciding to make the most of her amusement. "I haven't tasted anything so awful since I was fifteen and Knobby Nelson made up a batch of hooch in a rusty washtub out behind his dad's barn."

"Barn?" Lisa repeated. "Are you a country boy, for all your worldly sophistication?"

"Right out of an Iowa cornfield," Pete said, amazed that Lisa would refer to *his* worldly sophistication—especially after the performance he'd just given. Was she making fun of him? He didn't think so, but a tiny, annoyingly cynical part of him couldn't be sure.

He wished he'd kept his mouth shut about where he'd come from. Not that he wanted his background to be a secret, but there was nothing in it to interest someone like Lisa Sinclair. "You know, I'd like a decent cognac," he said with a slightly forced smile. "But not here, for obvious reasons. Harry and Sheila Milton mentioned the other night that they haven't seen you, and they'd like to. They'll be going to a club down by the waterfront . . ." Pete's smile became more genuine. "The one where Harry told me he thought you'd turn up eventually. How about it, Lisa? Are you game?"

Lisa tried her very best to summon her resistance, knowing that every moment she spent with Pete Cochrane was undermining her common sense.

But she couldn't refuse. She just couldn't make herself do it. "Sure, I'm game," she said, convinced she was going to regret her decision.

When Gaston brought the check, he gave another of his courtly little half bows. "You will come back again soon, I hope. We are always most happy to see you, Mademoiselle Sinclair. And, *m'sieur*," he added with a wink, "our beautiful plant will look forward to your next visit."

Pete laughed and put enough francs down to cover the bill plus a healthy tip. "I like that guy," he said as he and Lisa left the restaurant.

"Gaston liked you too," Lisa said. "Otherwise he wouldn't have allowed himself his bit of fun." Only at that moment did it occur to Lisa that she'd never shared her special little café with anyone but Pete. It was her private haven.

She decided it was a good thing Pete was in town only for the few days of the jazz festival, because there was a slim chance that she could hold onto her heart for just about that long.

Five

The piano bar's owner-performer spied Lisa as soon as she and Pete had stepped inside the club. "Coo, Lisa! I ain't seen you in a dog's age," he said without stumbling over his arpeggio. "Come on in, luv, an' yer mate too." With a wave of his head that didn't disturb the long ash on the cigarette dangling from his mouth, Johnny Carlos indicated an empty spot just big enough for two in the corner to his right.

"Wait till Johnny finds out who my mate is," Lisa said as she and Pete headed for the table. "He's a big fan of yours. But he must have told you already; Johnny tends to gush."

"He doesn't recognize me, as far as I know," Pete said, happily deciding that Lisa was a bigger fan of his than Johnny Carlos or anyone else could possibly be. She seemed to think everybody was familiar with that obscure *Manhattan Concerto* album.

As he pulled back the table to let Lisa slip into the burgundy velvet armchair behind it, he noticed a number of male gazes directed her way. He wasn't surprised; even in this city filled with international beauties, Lisa was special, her tailored outfit more sensuous than the outrageously provocative dresses of several other women, her shining, bobbed hair sexier than all the luxuriant tresses that spilled with artful carelessness over bare shoulders, her slender grace more exciting than the most voluptuous curves.

But he didn't like the bold attention directed at her, his long-dormant male territorialism suddenly rearing its head, surprising him with its ferocity.

"Johnny's not a bad musician," Lisa said. "He's not in your league, of course. He plays mainly for background, not for close attention, but he's pleasant enough to listen to."

"Johnny Carlos," Pete said with a grin, relaxing a little. "A French pianist with a name that's half Spanish, and an English accent that's half cockney? What's his gimmick?"

Lisa smiled. "Johnny's like a lot of people here—a very mixed breed. He's a Londoner of Italian-Spanish origin, with a soft spot for things American and an abiding appreciation for the sights of the Côte d'Azur beaches." Especially those of the topless variety, she thought, wondering with a prickle of irritation whether Pete, like most night-owl musicians, spent his free afternoons enjoying viewing the nubile young things who bounced along the strand wearing one-piece bikinis. He did appear to be acquiring a bit of a tan, she'd noticed.

"I can't say I blame Johnny," Pete said with a grin, realizing what sights Lisa was referring to. But acres of anonymous breasts weren't his idea of erotic stimulation. He preferred more private, personal encounters, such as that kiss in Lisa's office. He smiled at her, looking longingly at her delicious mouth, thinking about the kisses he had yet to savor.

"Do you mind if I introduce him to you?" Lisa asked hastily, acutely aware of the direction of Pete's thoughts.

"Introduce him?" Pete echoed blankly, then shook his head. "Oh, you mean Johnny. Why should I mind meeting a fan? I'm far from jaded by the experience, believe me."

Lisa was beginning to believe that Pete's modesty was genuine. But perhaps it was justified in terms of his not being recognized. As his student admirer at the festival had demonstrated, Pete himself wasn't known, but his style was. His music had managed to become popular without much publicity about the man—which was, she suspected, a mistake. Pete could capitalize on his good looks, though she rather admired that he chose not to.

Lisa perused those good looks while he gave the waiter their orders for cognac. Pete was gorgeous, she decided anew; there simply wasn't any way around that fact. The man's very imperfections, if they could be termed imperfections, only enhanced his attractiveness: the dark brows, almost too heavy and straight; the deep-set eyes suggesting a hidden, introspective nature; the nose and chin bordering on being too strong; the wonderful mouth that tended to curve into a brilliant smile so often and so easily, and with such devastating effect.

Lisa remembered how that mouth had felt moving over hers, gently persuasive one minute, hard and demanding the next, creating coils of heat deep inside her. . . .

Stop it! she ordered herself.

Realizing that the waiter was gone and Pete was

giving her a rather curious look, Lisa groped for some way to explain the way she'd been staring at him. "You . . . you seem to be acquiring a bit of a tan," she said at last, reverting to her earlier thought. "I suppose you've spent a few afternoons on the beach." But that subject was a mistake, she quickly discovered as she began picturing him in nothing but a narrow strip of cloth, his broad chest becoming a deep, warm bronze in the brilliant Mediterranean sun.

"If I'm getting a tan, it must be from spending so much time outdoors sight-seeing. I'm not much of a sunbather," Pete said, watching Lisa's incredibly expressive eyes, wishing he knew what was going on behind them, suspecting he had a pretty fair idea. "Besides, the beach here isn't very inviting. It's too rocky. Even with the cushions they lie on, I can't understand how all those scantily clad girls keep from getting their—from cutting themselves to ribbons. Or at least acquiring some bruises along with their bikini lines."

"Their precious *few* bikini lines," Lisa murmured with a demure smile.

Pete didn't quite succeed at suppressing a grin; he relished the thought that the glints in Lisa's velvety eyes were burning with a different kind of light, that there was an interesting feline streak in her.

He couldn't resist taking her hand to raise the tips of her fingers to his lips, releasing her only when the waiter arrived with their snifters of cognac.

Lisa was shaken by the gentle caress. It took her straight back to her office, and to the moment of intimacy with Pete that had been unlike any she'd known before. She seriously wondered if she would ever be able to work peacefully in that office again.

Johnny Carlos finished his piano set and stood up, his cigarette still dangling, the ash a good half-inch-long and curving precariously downward. After waving to a few of the bar's patrons and stopping briefly to chat here and there, he approached Lisa and Pete. "Wot's 'appenin', luv?" he asked as he got down on his haunches beside the small table, balancing on his toes. "Where've you been lately?"

"Working, mainly," Lisa answered. "I'd like you to meet my friend Pete." She grinned as Johnny casually thrust out his hand to Pete. "Pete Cochrane, Johnny Carlos."

"Right, well, it's—" Johnny's head suddenly snapped around as he gaped at Lisa, his hand still grasping Pete's. "Y'mean Pete Cochrane? The very one?"

"The very one," Lisa answered, her lips twitching with amusement.

The ash finally dropped into Johnny's lap. He didn't notice. "As I live and breathe, Pete Cochrane!" He began pumping Pete's hand as if trying to coax water out of a stubborn well. "Pleased t' meet yer, mate! Lisa never told me you wuz a chum of 'ers."

"Pete and I met on my last trip to New Orleans," Lisa explained.

"Blimey, Pete—y' don't mind if I calls y' Pete? Yer playin' in the festival?"

"No," Pete said in answer to both questions, at the same time trying in vain to retrieve his hand. "I'm just here as a tourist."

"T' think I've been sittin' there at the piano wiv you in my audience. Say, Pete, would y' giv' us a number? I'd be honored, I would."

Pete finally managed to extricate his hand from

the other man's grip. "That's generous of you, Johnny, but I'd really prefer not to. To tell the truth, I've been enjoying listening to your work. I'd just as soon let you carry on."

Beaming with obvious pride, Johnny gave an understanding nod. "Well, I guess a man on 'oliday deserves to be let alone, don't he? But tell me, Pete, is there another album comin' along? I've fair worn out yer first."

"Some time in the next few months I should have a new one out," Pete answered. Lisa had been right, he thought with slightly embarrassed pleasure: Johnny did tend to gush. "May I buy you a drink, Johnny?"

"Thanks anyway, mate, but I don't indulge while on the job." Johnny stared at Pete for a moment, as if absorbing that his hero was real. "So we can look forward to some new Pete Cochrane work, can we?" he finally said. Then, without waiting for an answer, he launched into an enthusiastic commentary on the touches of genius he'd discovered in every number on Pete's first album.

As Lisa sat back and listened to the two men—or rather, to Johnny—she was impressed by Pete's unwavering graciousness, and she began doubting seriously that she could keep her feelings under control for so much as another hour, much less ten days— should it prove necessary. Pete wasn't merely attractive, talented, and devastatingly sexy: he was fun to be with. A down-to-earth, likable man. He would, she suspected, grow on a woman until ultimately he had inspired utter devotion from her.

Too easily, she saw herself as that adoring woman.

But even if he were to care for her, and even if there were time for a romance to bloom, there could be no future for her with Pete Cochrane. It wouldn't work out, if only for logistic reasons. The Atlantic lay between them, not to mention two highly demanding careers.

Pete was becoming uncomfortable. Johnny's endless flattery was a bit much, and watching the man remain poised on his haunches was enough to give a person sympathetic leg cramps.

But what bothered Pete most was that Lisa's intense scrutiny was arousing responses in him that didn't belong in a public place. He wasn't sure how much more of her warm, caressing gaze he could take without succumbing to the insane urge to carry her off to some secret grotto.

At last, Johnny did a jack-in-the-box spring to a standing position. "I see me lady friend has arrived. She's late, just like a woman. An' all alone, so I'd better go give 'er a kiss before some other bloke starts gettin' ideas. See y' later, Pete. I'll be watchin' for that album." With a rakish wink at Lisa, Johnny moved away.

After he'd left, Lisa smiled at Pete. "Didn't I tell you Johnny was a fan?"

Pete chuckled. "I could learn to like this neck of the woods. It gives my ego a real boost."

"Does your ego need a boost?"

"Doesn't everybody's?"

Lisa smiled. If there was a reason for Pete's modesty, he wasn't about to explain it to her. "I guess you have a point."

Glancing around the room, she recognized several people, but didn't see some of the friends she had expected would be there.

"Harry and Sheila should be showing up soon," Pete murmured, as if reading her thoughts.

"Is Sheila enjoying the trip?" Lisa asked, finally fastening upon a harmless subject. "It's her first time here."

"She's like a kid on Christmas morning," Pete answered, privately thinking the description suited the way he felt about being with Lisa.

"I'm so glad," Lisa said. "Sheila's a lovely . . ." Her words trailed off as she saw Johnny, back at the piano, shooting a glance at Pete and leaning forward to speak into the microphone. "Oh, dear," she whispered, hoping Pete wouldn't mind being the center of attention for a moment.

". . . And all you proper music lovers'll want to put yer 'ands together to say 'ello to Pete Cochrane, right over 'ere in the corner! Stand up, Pete! Take a bow!"

Expecting a smattering of tentative applause from puzzled patrons, Pete merely nodded, managing a grin. But he was startled as the crowd clapped heartily.

"C'mon, Pete!" Johnny badgered. "Don't be shy!"

"You'd better do it," Lisa said quietly. "I'm sorry I got you into this."

"Hey, it's great!" Pete said, scraping back his chair to stand up briefly. "Such is the price of fame," he added with a wink as he sat down again. But he felt like a fool. There were major jazz stars wandering around Nice, and here he was, not even part of the festival, being introduced as if he were a celebrity. Yet as he glanced about the room, he was surprised again by the continuing applause and the smiling faces.

"You still don't believe it," Lisa said. "You think these people are being polite. You're giving Johnny's coaxing the credit for the interest in you, not your own reputation."

To his private disgust, Pete felt the familiar heat of a blush rising over his face. He tossed back a healthy swig of cognac, then grinned. "Nah. This humble bit is part of my shtick. I already told you I know the French are crazy about me."

Lisa wasn't surprised that Pete was better known in France than in his own country. Musicians, especially jazz artists, often found acceptance more readily in Europe than in North America. What amazed her was that he truly seemed unaware of the extent of his growing popularity.

After a moment's thought, she realized why he didn't know how well received his work was. "Come to think of it, this groundswell of excitement about you really got going only within the last couple of months. You probably haven't even seen the sales figures. I think a local disc jockey who decided you should be a cult figure gets some of the credit."

"And are you, by any chance, a part-time disc jockey, Lisa?" Pete asked with a laugh. But he was almost serious, beginning to realize just how much she did think of his work. Gratified as he was by Lisa's admiration, Pete found himself wondering if his minor but growing fame was the main reason he appealed to her. She didn't seem like the kind of star junkie so many women he'd met had turned out to be, but he'd been burned a few times. Christine Michaels hadn't been the first lady who'd seemed to like him for himself, only to latch on to the first bigger fish who'd happened along. Christine had just been the last—or so he hoped.

With an effort, he laughed inwardly at his lingering insecurities. If lovely, classy Lisa Sinclair had wanted a major name as an escort, she could have found any number of willing candidates at the festival grounds.

Besides, he thought, he was getting a little ahead of himself, not to mention forgetting that he was the pursuer, and Lisa his very elusive quarry. There were times when the hang-ups of his youth made him ridiculously illogical, he thought. He had to fight those cynical tendencies of his.

Watching the play of emotions in Pete's eyes, Lisa found her curiosity getting the best of her. "Why are you this way, Pete? How can you play your music with such confidence and mastery, yet blush when you get a bit of recognition?"

At first, Pete wasn't sure how to respond. Then he remembered Lisa's own line. "It's a long story," he said with a grin. "I don't think I know you well enough to tell it to you."

It was Lisa's turn to blush. She realized she'd broken one of her own strict rules: She'd asked something that was none of her business. "I'm sorry," she said hastily. "I can't imagine what got into me. . . ."

"Of course, I wouldn't mind telling you my long story if we were to get to know each other a little better," Pete went on, grasping his opportunity. He took both her hands in his and spoke softly, persuasively. "I think I'd be willing to tell you just about anything, Lisa, if we knew each other better. What do you say we give it a try?"

Gazing into his blue eyes, Lisa couldn't remember even one of the excellent reasons why getting to know Pete Cochrane was a foolish thing to do.

Vaguely certain that she did have valid reasons, she tried and tried to recall them so she could explain their perfect logic.

Pete waited for her answer, wondering why she found it so difficult to choose one of two simple, tiny words.

Suddenly sensing another presence at the table, he looked up.

"I see you two have gotten together," Harry Milton said with a proud grin worthy of a professional matchmaker. His wife, Sheila, tall and slim with salt-and-pepper hair, looked on approvingly.

After an exchange of greetings, Pete stood up and glanced around the bar, searching for a larger table.

"We're not staying," Harry said. "We just came to meet some people to get the address for that drop-in party Charlene Lee invited the entire South of France to."

Turning to Lisa, Pete raised his brow questioningly. He hadn't thought about taking her to Charlene's party. It would be noisy and crowded. Worse, he would face some very heavy competition there for her attention.

On the other hand, he thought, if he could talk her into going with him, perhaps he could stretch their evening together into the wee hours. He did like that possibility.

The party's host was a superrich industrialist who'd been squiring Charlene Lee since he'd caught her nightclub act in Las Vegas a few months earlier. The huge bash was being held in his reputedly magnificent villa on the outskirts of Nice. It wouldn't hurt to be able to take Lisa to where she would meet her own kind of people—the rich and titled and famous she probably figured an ordinary Yank like Pete Cochrane wouldn't know.

A nagging inner voice told him to quit trying to win Lisa by impressing her. It wasn't his style to put on the dog for any woman. But he couldn't seem to help himself. "This shindig should be fun," he said casually, then dropped the names of a few top jazz stars who were supposed to be going to the party.

Lisa hesitated, feeling a little like Cinderella with pumpkin time approaching. She knew she should end the evening at this point, while she still held on to a few shreds of sense.

But before she could speak, Sheila piped up. "Please say you'll come, Lisa. It would be nice to see a familiar face for a change. I find I know so few of the other women at these get-togethers."

Lisa needed no further rationalization for doing what she wanted to do anyway. "Well, naturally I'd love to go," she said, then remembered something she ought to explain. "I should tell you, though, I—"

"So it's settled," Harry interrupted, waving to someone across the room. "And there are our people now. I'll go get the address, and the four of us can share a cab."

The next few minutes were taken up with Pete paying the check while Sheila chatted excitedly to Lisa about the shopping she'd been doing from Monte Carlo to St.-Tropez.

In the taxi, all the talk was centered on the performances of the festival.

Lisa never did get a chance to make her explanation. And, to her dismay, they hadn't been inside the palatial cypress-guarded villa five minutes before it became unnecessary.

Pete was taken aback by the way Charlene Lee was making a beeline for him, her arms outstretched in an enthusiastic welcome, her crimson lips widening in a huge smile. Harry and Sheila, who knew Charlene much better than he did, had spied a couple of friends and had gone to speak to them, so there was no mistaking the object of Charlene's effusive greeting. But it was puzzling.

He bent his head to speak quietly to Lisa, hoping to explain hastily that Charlene was only an acquaintance, that he had no idea why the woman was being so friendly. He didn't want Lisa to get the wrong idea. "That lady in the slinky red dress, the one who's about to descend on us—I suppose you recognize her. She's—"

"You *did* come!" Charlene cried, breezing past Pete to swoop down on Lisa with a typically French embrace, kissing the air and almost touching both Lisa's cheeks, disturbing not so much as a grain of powder on the singer's face or one sleek black hair on her head. "I haven't seen you for ages, Lisa! I was so hoping you'd be here tonight, but my secretary said you'd called to tell me you probably wouldn't make it." Grasping Lisa's upper arms and stepping back to survey her, Charlene shook her head. "Lord, honey, you look better every time I see you. How have you been? I hear great things about that travel company you and those fabulous sisters of yours operate."

Lisa smiled nervously, wishing she'd had an opportunity to tell Pete about the note she'd received from Charlene earlier in the week inviting her to the party. "You're looking pretty terrific yourself, Char," she said, hoping Pete didn't think she'd kept him in the dark deliberately. She glanced approvingly over her longtime friend's silk-sheathed, statuesque form. "You always were meant for these Lagerfeld gowns. And I've been keeping a scrapbook of your press clippings so I can tell my future grandchildren that I knew Charlene Lee when." With what she hoped was a modicum of poise, Lisa indicated Pete. "You two know each other, don't you?"

"Of course," Charlene said warmly, turning to give Pete a perfunctory hug. "Chicago, wasn't it? Club appearances in the same hotel?"

"San Francisco," Pete murmured, his surprise tempered by sardonic amusement. "But what are a few thousand miles between friends? Congratulations on your new video, by the way. It's great stuff."

Charlene beamed at him. "To be perfectly honest, I'm rather pleased with it myself. Now, why don't you two come with me out back? That's where the action is. But I warn you, Pete, I'll want to steal Lisa for a while. This lady was one of the first people to encourage me to give the music business an honest try instead of going home to be a singing teacher in Rutland, Vermont. For some reason, we've been having a hard time getting together lately, so we're overdue for a catch-up session of girl talk. You won't mind, will you?"

"Of course not," Pete lied, though he wanted Lisa all to himself. He was more and more intrigued by her. Besides, he was a little worried about what was ahead, wondering if he could hold her interest in the midst of such a glittering crowd.

"Guess who feels sheepish *now*," he whispered to Lisa as Charlene led them through the airy, high-ceilinged rooms toward open glass doors at the rear of the villa.

"I wanted to explain that I'd been invited," she said in a low voice, "but there wasn't time. Honestly, I wasn't doing a number on you, Pete."

He winked at her. "I know, Lisa. You're not that

kind of person. But I'll bet I feel a lot sillier about my name-dropping than you did about translating Côte d'Azur."

The area Charlene had referred to so casually as "out back" reminded Pete of a minor Taj Mahal with its long, rectangular turquoise pool, over which loomed a colonnaded structure that might have been an actual Greek temple in some long-distant past. The grounds, enclosed by a low stone wall overgrown with artistically planted flowers and shrubs, commanded a panoramic view of both the port of Nice and the Bay of Angels beyond. Lush grass was dotted by marble statues and white wrought-iron tables, chairs, and lounges, the umbrellas and chair paddings a sunny yellow and occupied by guests who reeked of wealth. "Not a bad little joint," Pete murmured.

Hearing Pete's remark, Charlene turned and grinned at him. "It's a long way from Chicago, isn't it?"

"San Francisco," he said with a smile.

As Pete lifted two glasses of champagne from a passing waiter's silver tray, Charlene waved over his shoulder. "Frankie, look who's here! And you said she wasn't coming!"

The lanky, red-bearded man Pete recognized as a trombonist in a television talk show band made his way over and gave Lisa a bear hug. "If it isn't the Bora Bora baby herself," he said, then kissed her cheek with a resounding smack.

Pete scowled as he handed Lisa one of the crystal flutes. "Bora Bora baby?"

Embarrassed by all the attention, Lisa accepted the champagne gratefully. "That's where I was born," she explained after taking a tiny sip. "Bora Bora."

"Oh. Bora Bora. Of course," Pete said vaguely, having a little trouble absorbing everything.

The remainder of the time Pete and Lisa spent at the party followed along much the same lines, and the festivities began deteriorating for him very quickly as he gradually reached the unhappy conclusion that his background and Lisa's were worlds apart.

Not only had Lisa known Charlene since their college days together, she was also on a first-name basis with the wealthy industrialist owner of the villa, and many of the guests—including several top musicians, a sex-symbol French film hero, a well-known German tycoon, and a titled Englishman who showed more than a passing interest in her.

Pete found himself fighting old demons, feeling like a hick in city clothes, a near success who hadn't quite figured out how to thrust through some invisible barrier to reach the big time—and not certain he wanted to get there. Even the compliments suddenly being heaped on him by fellow musicians and an apparently growing following of fans were small comfort when he kept seeing himself as a kid on the sidelines of a game he hadn't been asked to play, when he kept hearing his father's voice saying, "You're ridin' for a fall, Peter Cochrane. Learnin' fancy foreign languages won't get you a job, and makin' up songs won't earn you a livin'. That schoolteacher of yours had no business fillin' your head with big ideas and lettin' you waste your lunch hours at the piano. It was no favor she did you, boy. No favor at all."

Pete's dark mood wasn't lightened by the way Lisa kept being whisked away from him by one or another of her old friends, not by the fact that she didn't seem to mind wandering off to chat with this smooth-mannered marquess or that famous actor.

At one point, persuading himself to stop being so supersensitive, Pete made his way toward a spot just behind Lisa, intending to think of some winning way to steal her from the clutches of a white-haired man who'd been talking to her much longer than Pete liked.

As Pete drew close to the pair, he stopped in his tracks.

"The prince must see you, Lisa darling," the would-be silver fox was saying, his eyes devouring Lisa. "You are so much like our dear late Princess Grace in her glorious prime, it is uncanny. Let me take you to that opera ball in Monte Carlo. You will be the sensation of the evening, I promise you."

Pete felt as if he'd stepped into some weird dream. Or perhaps onto a movie set. The prince? Princess Grace? He scowled. Lisa didn't look like Grace Kelly. She looked like Lisa. Which wasn't bad at all.

But what woman could resist such lines from a man? Such extravagant compliments? What woman wouldn't jump at the chance to go to a ball in Monte Carlo to catch the eye of a prince?

And who could measure up to that kind of competition?

Pete moved away from the pair, spying a clarinetist buddy of his who looked equally uncomfortable in the crowd.

Catching sight of Pete from the corner of her eye, Lisa wondered why he'd walked right by instead of stopping to rescue her from the name-dropping bore she couldn't seem to shake. She certainly hadn't expected Pete to hover over her throughout the party, especially when he could enjoy the rare chance to be with fellow musicians, and perhaps even bask in the glow of some of the flattery undoubtedly being heaped upon him. But a little attention from the man who'd brought her to this stupid party would have been nice, she thought. Of course, coming there hadn't been his idea, she suddenly realized. He hadn't suggested it until Harry had brought it up.

She couldn't help wondering why. Was there another woman at the party, someone else Pete had been romancing? Was he in the awkward position that sometimes befell handsome bachelors who couldn't keep their date books sorted out?

"Say it, lovely Lisa," her companion was urging her. "Say you'll decorate my arm at the ball."

Lisa gave him a careful smile. She was a businesswoman, she reminded herself. The wealthy social set she'd drifted into, simply by knowing people like Charlene Lee "when," had turned out to be invaluable to the rapid success of Dreamweavers. Contacts were vital, so she had to be pleasant to everyone, even to phonies like this Gunther person who'd managed to mention his Swiss bank account half a dozen times within the first five minutes of meeting her. "I'm sorry," she murmured. "I'm afraid the duke has already booked me for the ball. You will excuse me, won't you? I see the countess giving me the high sign." Spying the tall form and silver-streaked hair of Sheila Milton, Lisa made her way through the crush and sighed with relief when she reached the older woman.

"Who was that distinguished man you were talking to?" Sheila asked.

Lisa laughed. "I'm not sure who he is, but he thinks you're a countess and I have a shot at landing a duke. Where's Harry?"

"Oh, he's off in a corner comparing gigs with the boys in the band," Sheila said. "Why does that fellow think I'm a countess?"

"Because he wants to," Lisa said, suppressing a sigh. She realized she shouldn't have come to this party. When Pete had suggested it, she should have remembered what happened to Cinderellas who tried to prolong an evening with Prince Charming.

At the moment, Lisa thought, sweeping out a fireplace would be better than hanging around this particular palace.

She started considering the possibilites for a graceful exit. It was just about time to make one.

Six

Pete gradually became aware of the curvaceous but rather predictable starlet who'd started chattering to him at some point during the past few minutes—he wasn't sure when. Smiling vaguely at the girl, Pete couldn't help wondering if she would be more his speed than Lisa Sinclair. He hoped not.

From across the room, noting Pete's little tête-à-tête with a girl who seemed to have mislaid half her dress somewhere, Lisa decided she'd had it with the whole scene. She was thoroughly annoyed with herself. Hadn't she known better than to go soft over a man? Especially a musician?

She realized with sickening clarity that she was suffering from infuriating, garden-variety jealousy. It was an emotion she had no respect for, and one she hadn't experienced often, for the simple reason that she didn't allow herself to become involved enough with any man to care what he did or with whom he did it.

But she did care about Pete Cochrane. And what

was most disturbing about her feeling for him was that it went beyond physical desire.

How had she allowed such a thing to happen?

"Hey, Lisa, you've finally turned up," Colette's leather-clad drummer said as he sidled over to her.

"Where's Colette?" Lisa asked, not even trying to smile politely.

"Colette? Who knows? She doesn't answer to me any more than I answer to her. She doesn't own me."

"But when I talked to her this afternoon," Lisa said coldly, "Colette was under the impression that she had a date with you tonight."

"Well, then, she was wrong, wasn't she! I'm a free man, Lisa. Free to cheer you up—and you look like a lady who needs cheering up."

"Indeed I am," Lisa said as she moved away from him without a backward glance.

Musicians, she thought, almost growling the word aloud.

She managed to slalom past all obstacles to reach Pete, pasting on a smile just as The Bosom giggled adorably at some remark he'd made.

"I don't want to be a wet blanket," Lisa said, proud of how unconcerned she sounded, "but I've had all the partying I can absorb." She kept her expression bland, even favoring the starlet with a pseudofriendly smile. "There's no need for me to interrupt, though. I can call a cab or hitch a ride with a friend."

With a friend, Pete thought, his stomach twisting into knots. He was tempted to tell Lisa to go ahead and climb into the nearest limo and be whisked home in the lap of the luxury to which she obviously was accustomed. But his Iowa upbringing wouldn't allow it. "I brought you here," he said pleasantly but firmly. "I'll take you home."

"Will you come back, Petey?" the starlet asked in a simpering voice.

Pete almost grimaced. Why were the attainable women such dopes and the unattainable ones so . . . so unattainable? He smiled at the girl. "I don't think so, Poppy." Even her name struck him as absurd, though he suspected if it were Lisa's name, he would think it the most beautiful one he'd ever heard. A wicked impulse gripped him, and he pointed to the white-haired lothario who'd asked Lisa to the big Monte Carlo show-and-tell. "Listen, Poppy," Pete said in a confidential tone, "that fellow over there has been giving you the eye all evening. I think you should go and say hello to him. I understand he arrived here on his yacht." Every word was true, Pete thought, justifying himself. The guy had been drooling over several women at the party. If Lisa was interested in him, she ought to be told what kind of womanizer he was.

Lisa suppressed a smile. Obviously Pete had spotted Gunther What's-His-Name for a phony.

Once Poppy had made a beeline for bigger game, Pete cupped his hand around Lisa's elbow. "Shall we go find a phone?"

Lisa nodded. "I didn't mean to spoil your fun," she said, not especially comforted by Pete's apparent lack of interest in Poppy. There were always more women where that one had come from. Lots more.

Pete said nothing. He didn't want to admit he hadn't been having fun. A person was supposed to have fun at such a glamorous party. A person wasn't supposed to brood about not belonging there, about not wanting to be there, about aching for a woman he shouldn't have been attracted to in the first place. "Should we find our host and hostess and say good night?" he asked after he'd phoned for a taxi.

"In this crush, I think it would be impossible," Lisa answered. "I'll send Charlene a note tomorrow. I'll thank her for both of us."

"Good idea," he said. "Do you want to wait outside for the cab?"

Lisa nodded. "It would help, yes."

Pete looked sharply at her. "Help what?"

My throbbing headache, Lisa wanted to tell him. "Nothing, really," she said aloud. "It's just that the noise and the smoke are getting to me. The fresh air would be lovely."

The night was redolent of lush summer flowers, palm trees sighed as a cool breeze caressed them, and the moonlight spilled over Lisa like sprinkled gold dust.

Pete ached to take her in his arms and just hold her. But she stood quietly, as still as the pale statues that dotted the villa grounds, her body stiff and erect, her chin high, her smile as frozen as the curved lips that had been chiseled in marble two thousand years before.

She was going to be regally polite right to the bitter end of the evening if it killed her, Pete thought. The tension didn't ease during the taxi ride. "Where are you staying?" Lisa asked, breaking the uncomfortable silence.

When Pete told her the name of his hotel, she nodded, assuming her business manners as if they were armor. "We'll have to pass your hotel before we get to my neighborhood," she said briskly. "I live up in the Cimiez area, so it's silly for you to go all the way there and have to double back."

Pete stared at her, then narrowed his eyes. "Lisa, I don't know what kind of gentlemen you usually hang around with in that diamond-studded crowd of yours, but this corn-fed Midwesterner grew up with the idea that a fellow sees a girl right to her door. Especially at this hour of the morning."

Lisa swallowed hard, realizing she'd offended him. "I see," she murmured, suddenly feeling very sad and wishing their brief encounter could have ended more happily. "Well, that's . . . very kind of you."

Pete let out a little snort. "Right. Very kind," he muttered, hating the way things had turned out, hating himself even more.

True to his word, he went into her apartment building and all the way to her door after telling the cab to wait.

As Lisa fitted her key into the lock, she realized she couldn't bear saying good-bye to Pete without mentioning the tension that had come between them. "Why are you so angry with me?" she asked in a small voice. "I didn't ask you to leave the party. I didn't even ask to go to it in the first place. Or particularly want to."

Pete was taken aback by Lisa's directness. And she was right, he realized. He *was* angry with her. But the instant he recognized his bitterness, seeing it for the useless, unfair emotion it was, it disappeared. "I guess it rankles me that you're out of my reach," he answered honestly, then curved his hands around her shoulders and pressed a gentle kiss to her forehead. "But I have no right to be mad at you for things you have no control over. So I'm sorry. I could have been more gracious about the whole thing."

Lisa stared up at him in shock. Out of his reach? Had he picked up on the emotional paralysis she managed to keep hidden from everyone else? He was a sensitive person; it was quite possible he'd realized intuitively that a long time ago—years before a passing sax player had wounded her feelings and her pride—she'd lost the courage and the will to let anyone get too close to her.

On the other hand, she thought, Pete might be just another roving musician who'd decided he could have a better time at the festival with a more willing lady.

She remembered how she'd kissed him earlier in the evening, how she'd looked at him, wanted him. She almost laughed. How willing did she have to *be*? But perhaps the problem was the opposite: Had she been *too* willing? Did Pete require a more challenging chase before the final conquest?

As she looked at him, she couldn't accept that he was so shallow. She couldn't believe it of him. She focused on her original thought: Pete had seen through her. He knew she couldn't let down the creaking drawbridge that protected her heart.

It struck Lisa that she was subjecting herself to the kind of self-questioning, inner debates she'd vowed never to get involved in again. They were absolutely nonproductive, as her mother would put it.

After taking a deep breath, she managed to say the only thing she could be certain she sincerely felt: "I'm sorry if I've hurt your feelings, Pete. I wouldn't, you know. Not on purpose. Not for the world."

Pete's hands tightened on her shoulders. He'd been wavering, unable to leave her, asking himself whether what Harry Milton had warned him about—his reverse snobbishness—had reared its ugly head.

But Lisa's words, so simple and so obviously heartfelt, touched him more deeply than he dared let her see. Even the way she said his name in her low, velvety voice tugged at his heart. Unable to speak past a sudden lump in his throat, he simply kissed her forehead again, released her, mumbled vague good-bye, and hurried away, not even sure where he was going.

For the second time since she'd met Pete, Lisa was overwhelmed by a sense of terrible loss, a feeling that she was committing some dreadful mistake.

But this time, she reminded herself, it wasn't her mistake. Pete was the one who was bolting.

She knew now how she'd made him feel in New Orleans.

When Lisa turned up at the office early the next morning, unable to sleep late despite her best efforts, she was surprised to hear Colette whistling lustily as she typed invoices—the woman's least favorite chore.

"You seem to be in a good mood this morning," Lisa said, carefully watching the receptionist's reaction, suspecting a bit of bravado. Surely Colette was slightly hurt by her drummer's defection.

"I'm in a terrific mood this morning," Colette said cheerfully. "I met the most charming young man last night. He's one of yours."

"One of mine?" Lisa said, raising her brow.

"An American. From Los Angeles. He's a student and he's adorable."

"What happened to your *adorable* drummer?" Lisa asked, choosing not to mention that she'd seen him at the villa party.

Colette wrinkled her nose. "He turned out to be not so adorable. I had dinner with him last night, just the way we'd planned, but by the time we got to the crème caramel, I wanted to dump it over his head. He's too full of himself for my taste. So I told him I had to go home and wash my hair, and then *I* paid for the meal—you see, Lisa, I do listen to your funny little lectures about integrity—and I left before the coffee arrived. I met my American three blocks away. He walked me home, and I'm taking him over to Monte Carlo tonight to play the slots at the casino. He said he's always wanted to do that." Colette smiled dreamily. "He's so sweet."

Lisa was chuckling and shaking her head by the end of the tale. "You know, Colette," she said, still laughing as she picked up her mail and went into her own office, "you're a tonic. You really are."

By midafternoon, Lisa's lack of sleep was catching up with her. Glad she'd worn her favorite outfit—an easy-fitting, ivory pantsuit made from a fabric that refused to wrinkle, and a cool, comfortable black silk shell—she decided to steal a little nap. She poked her head out into the reception area. "Colette, could you hold my calls? I'm not here, all right?"

"You got it," Colette said.

Lisa frowned. "You got it?"

The girl giggled. "My American says that all the time. He's such a darling!"

Shaking her head again, Lisa closed her office door, hung her jacket in the closet, kicked off her shoes, and stretched out on the Louis XV chaise that was more decorative than comfortable, but was adequate for a bit of shut-eye.

The next thing she knew, Colette was crouched beside her, whispering her name.

Lisa leapt up to a sitting position as if she'd been wakened by a thunderclap, her heart pounding, her thoughts confused. For a moment, she almost imagined she was back in her tiny cabin on the *Dream-weaver*, the rest of the family up on deck as the sailing vessel scudded over the waters of the South Pacific.

"Oh, dear, now that was what I was trying not to do," Colette said, scowling as she got to her feet. "I thought I should wake you to tell you I'm leaving now, but I didn't want to startle you. You really should do something about your nerves, Lisa."

Gradually Lisa realized she wasn't aboard the *Dreamweaver*, wasn't a child who'd fallen asleep over a book, wasn't sobbing into her pillow about another temporary best friend she'd said good-bye to at the last port of call and probably would never see again.

How she hated reliving those sad moments in her sleep. "It's all right," she said, massaging the bridge of her nose with her thumb and forefinger. "I'm fine."

"Do you have nightmares often?" Colette asked.

Lowering her hand, Lisa stiffened and stared at the girl. "Did I seem to be having a nightmare?"

"You were whimpering, Lisa."

Forcing a laugh, Lisa told a substitute story to cover her embarrassment about the real one. "I was dreaming about the time Morgan decided to test herself to see if she'd cured her fear of snakes. I actually saw my crazy sister let a python wrap itself around her body, and I was sure it would constrict any minute and crush her. I guess you came in just as Cuddles—that was what Morgan called the creature, believe it or not—was looking at me with her beady little eyes, as if to say it was my turn next."

Colette's eyes widened. "No wonder you were whimpering! Did that really happen?"

"What Morgan did really happened, yes," Lisa said. "But I think my imagination must have added the last part. I don't suppose Cuddles was the least bit interested in me. And believe me, the feeling was mutual. Now, did you say something about leaving? How long did I sleep?"

"About two hours," Colette said as she returned to her own office. "Why don't you go home now?"

"I think I'll go for a walk," Lisa said, getting to her feet. She slipped into her shoes, went to the closet to get her jacket, then had her usual skirmish with her desk drawer to retrieve her black handbag. She was ready to leave with Colette.

"What a strange life you've had," Colette said on the way downstairs. "Traveling from one remote place to another, never knowing whether you were going to live in a primitive village or a quiet university town or an exotic city most of us only read about. Was it wonderful or horrible?"

"Mostly wonderful," Lisa said. She hesitated, tempted to open up a little. But loyalty to the parents she adored made it impossible for her to admit that any aspect of her early life hadn't been perfect. "I wouldn't trade my childhood for anyone else's," she finally said with total honesty. "I guess that's what counts." As they reached the street, Lisa chose not to go Colette's way. A long, solitary walk seemed to be in order. "Have fun with your American," she said, then added teasingly, "But remember, being from the City of Angels doesn't give a fellow celestial intentions."

"Who wants a saint?" Colette shot back as she waved to Lisa. "See you tomorrow."

Lisa headed for the pedestrian mall, deciding to do some window-shopping. Not five minutes had passed before she'd run into Harry Milton. Since most visitors spent quite a bit of time on the mall, Lisa wasn't surprised to find Harry there, but it shocked her that seeing him gave her a pang, simply because he was Pete's friend. "Hi," she managed with a cheerful smile. "Where's Sheila?"

"Buying out a few more stores," Harry answered. "And I was just looking for a place to have a beer. Will you join me?"

Lisa hesitated, then nodded. "I'd love a beer, Harry. There's a nice little sidewalk café just around the corner. But I'm buying, all right? There's something I'd like to pick your brains about, if you'll let me."

Harry grinned. "Something or someone?"

"Obviously I'm not going to have to stumble over any embarrassing preambles," Lisa said with a laugh. "How well do you know Pete Cochrane anyway?"

Half an hour later, Lisa was shaking her head in amazement. "I had no idea Pete might have been feeling defensive about my upper-crust friends, Harry. And I must admit I've been so quick to judge the musicians who collect groupies, I've been utterly blind to the possibility some musicians might be weary of being collected." She took a sip of her beer, then laughed quietly. "How can two people manage to stir up such a mess of misunderstandings in so short a time?"

Harry chuckled, took a sip of his beer, then motioned to the waiter for the check. "When the emotions get hot, the brains get fricasseed," he said to Lisa.

She gave him a bemused smile. "Is that an old Spanish proverb, Harry?"

"Nope. That's Milton. Harold, not John." Harry reached into his pocket for his wallet.

"I told you I'd buy," Lisa said, grabbing the check. "If you don't let me, I'll never trust you again."

He laughed and gave in. "Independent women," he muttered. "I love 'em. Now, if we can just find my independent lady and drag her away from these stores, a bunch of us are going to have dinner and then go on to another bash. A smaller one this time, not as fancy as last night's do. This one's just a matter of a few friends getting together to jam in a private little after-hours club. How about coming along, Lisa?"

"Will Pete be at dinner? At the party?" she asked bluntly.

"He's been invited," Harry answered with a shrug. "Whether or not he'll turn up is anybody's guess. Pete didn't seem to be in the best of moods when I saw him earlier today. But why do you ask? It seems to me that being an independent woman involves more than just picking up checks."

Lisa narrowed her eyes at Harry, then couldn't help smiling. The man knew exactly how to get to her, she thought fondly. "Count me in," she said. "But if Pete does join us, I think I might be sorry I picked up that gauntlet you just threw down."

"I have a feeling," Harry said, "you might be far sorrier if you hadn't."

At dinner, it was soon obvious that Lisa needn't have worried. Pete didn't arrive. And the aching emptiness his absence created in her was disturbing.

Nevertheless, she went on to the party with the others, deciding that Harry had been right: she couldn't let her foolish infatuation with Pete Cochrane run—or ruin—her life. She had to go out and have a good time, the way she always did during the jazz festival.

The jam session was in full swing by the time Harry's contingent arrived. Surreptitiously Lisa scanned the dim, smoky basement room that was the after-hours club. Pete wasn't there. She was disappointed, but the atmosphere was so lively she couldn't help getting into the spirit of things, and when one of her longtime buddies grabbed her by the hand to drag her over to the bongo drums that had been set up on a stand near the piano, she pushed up her jacket sleeves and got ready to cut loose.

Pete descended the stairway to join in on the informal jam session. He wasn't sure why he'd come, except that he'd decided it was stupid to stay away and end up brooding over what might have been.

He'd spent most of the day cursing his stupidity and wondering if there was any way to make amends with Lisa. It had been almost daylight when it had dawned on him that the jade glints he'd seen in Lisa's eyes at the end of the villa party had been sparks of jealousy. All the time he'd been nursing his poor-boy pride and jumping to the conclusion that Lisa had gravitated toward more likely candidates for her attention, she'd actually been getting riled about the starlet types like Poppy who'd helped him pass the time—and perhaps, he conceded, who'd soothed his overly fragile ego.

He'd picked up the phone at least a dozen times throughout the day, but there hadn't seemed much point in calling Lisa. He'd made a mess of things, and there was no way to go back and change the situation.

He only wished he could understand how a woman he'd known for such a short time could leave such a vacuum in his life.

Spotting Harry, Pete waved and started toward him, vaguely musing that the evening's music was rollicking along nicely. But he'd gone no more than four steps when he suddenly stopped, gaping in disbelief. The rollicker, the driving force behind a guitarist in a jazzy reggae number, was the pristine, cool, lovely Lisa—looking anything but pristine and cool, but lovelier than ever.

Pete was riveted to the spot, watching as she played the hottest bongo he'd heard in a long time, her eyes closed, a lock of her side-parted hair falling forward over her brow, her shoulders and hips moving just a little as she thumped out an intricate beat that had the whole crowd jumping.

The guitar player, a competent but not gifted musician, was having the time of his life, inspired by Lisa's pulsating, primitive rhythms, grinning blissfully at the unexpected earthiness of this delicate, pretty lady.

Pete surprised himself. Instead of being jealous, he was excited. Instead of grumbling inwardly that Lisa didn't seem to be too unhappy about what had happened the night before, he found himself charmed by her spunk.

An idea came to him. He and Lisa seemed to be best at nonverbal communication. Moving slowly toward the piano, he decided it was time, once again, to start communicating.

Lisa was lost in her own world, only dimly aware of the occasional "Oh, yeah!" and "Do it, baby!" from the crowd. In her imagination, she was on an island in Polynesia, and all around her people were feasting and dancing and laughing happily under a scorching sun and waving palm trees. The rhythms she played were some of the first sounds she'd heard in her life; her love of music had been imprinted vividly and early.

She was enjoying the melodies and harmonies the guitarist was choosing to put to her beat, but she couldn't help remembering how much more fun she'd had years earlier with a flute player and a ukulele virtuoso who'd been less involved with displaying their cleverness than with the sheer exhilaration of making music.

Then she heard a third sound. A light, teasing touch that suddenly brought the silent piano to scintillating life. As she opened her eyes, she knew instinctively what to expect, yet when she actually saw Pete smiling at her, looking fresh and magnetically virile, as if he'd just stepped out of a shower and into his white slacks and teal blue shirt, she barely managed to keep the rhythm going.

Remembering how Lisa had knocked him off his musical pins in New Orleans, Pete covered her lapse with a few bass runs that nudged her back to her uninhibited beat.

Lisa grinned as she realized what he was doing.

With their gazes locked, Lisa and Pete began finding each other's rhythms, discovering the nuances of movement and expression that signaled a shift in tempo, a change of mood. They barely noticed when the trio became a duet, the guitar player gradually backing off as, with a smile of unselfish pleasure, he saw that something special was happening that had nothing to do with him.

Pete and Lisa led each other a merry dance, first one and then the other experimenting with a playful improvisation or exploring a whole new direction. They ran the gamut from joyous musical spoofs on Caribbean favorites to spicy romantic ballads.

The crowd sometimes clapped to the beat, at other moments sat in rapt silence, at still others burst into spontaneous applause as a particularly clever bit of business or an especially soaring phrase caught their fancy. But they were far in the background for Pete and Lisa, shadowy figures in a world that had dwindled to just themselves.

Once again, as had happened in New Orleans and at the Cimiez festival grounds, Lisa felt as if Pete were making love to her. But this time she wasn't passively, reluctantly surrendering. This time she was his partner in seduction, not merely responding to him but demanding a response from him, giving as much as she took, taking as much as she gave. Her breath started coming in quick gasps, not because of the exertion—pounding out the rhythms of her innermost being seemed easy—but because of the heady exhilaration that had gripped her.

At last, Pete led her through a fast samba to a sexy bossa nova, and ended their little show with a recent salsa hit. He stood, strode over to Lisa, and wrapped his arms around her to lift her right off her feet and whirl her in a hug so exuberant, she was light-headed.

The crowd laughed and clapped and yelled for more, but Pete cheerfully refused. "It's somebody else's turn," he shouted over the din, then smiled at Lisa, still holding her above him. "What do you say we get out of here, squirt?"

She laughed, pretending to groan at the same time. "I thought you'd forgotten that awful nickname."

Letting her slide down until her feet touched the floor, then putting one arm around her shoulders, Pete tucked her in close to his side and guided her through the room to the stairway, both of them waving good-bye to Harry and Sheila.

When they were outside the club, Pete pulled Lisa into his arms again and, without warning, kissed her with all the heart-stopping, demanding urgency that had built up inside him during their erotically charged duet. He wasn't surprised when her full lips parted, when her tongue eagerly challenged his, when her body molded itself against him, creating a heat that set him on fire.

"What now, Lisa?" he murmured when he'd released her mouth long enough to struggle for breath.

"Let's go to my place," she said without hesitation. "We have so much to say to each other."

Burying his face in her silky, fragrant hair, Pete whispered, "I know, Lisa. There are all sorts of things I want to ask. I want to know everything about you." He laughed, then cradled her face in his hands and gazed down at her. "Starting with one question in particular," he said, smiling. "Where did you learn to play such a mean bongo?"

Lisa's eyes twinkled as she grinned back at him. "Why, in Bora Bora. Where else?"

Seven

With the aroma of freshly ground coffee wafting in from the kitchen along with the sound of Lisa's absentminded humming, Pete wandered around the living room of her apartment, picking up whatever bits of information her surroundings might reveal about her.

In some ways, her home confused him a little. Although the place was a perfect backdrop for Lisa's brand of feminine elegance—the pale peach walls, the shutters on the long, narrow windows painted a shade or two darker, the subtle lighting, the clean lines and pastel hues of the couch and chairs and tables—Pete couldn't help thinking fondly of the battered charm of Lisa's office furnishings. He wondered how she'd managed to decorate her apartment without succumbing to the mysterious character flaw that supposedly surfaced when she went furniture shopping.

Other things aroused Pete's curiosity as well. The biographies, art books, travel pictorials, and music histories came as no surprise, but Lisa's extensive collection of paperback thrillers and steamy best-sellers suggested unsuspected and intriguing facets of her personality. And while the soft-focus, pastoral watercolors on her walls were just right for the showroom-perfect decor, a group of startling masks and several earthy sculptures added an oddly attractive jarring note.

In the cab on the way to her place, Lisa had told Pete a bit about her childhood in the South Pacific, making it sound like something brought to life from a Gauguin painting, so the artifacts she'd acquired made perfect sense as sentimental souvenirs. Yet they were more than souvenirs. There was a primitive strength to them, a bold aggressiveness that excited Pete, the strangely painted faces and sensual shapes betraying the wildness he'd already glimpsed behind Lisa's cultivated facade.

He thought of the flickering emeralds in her almond-shaped eyes, the sleekness and grace of her body's movements, the explosive passion that was barely contained under her aloof surface. There was a streak of puma in his sophisticated lady, Pete mused, letting himself enjoy the mental image of Lisa arching her back in pleasure under his caressing hand, purring as she stroked her body against his.

When Lisa returned to the living room, Pete had to restrain himself from pouncing on her. "Nice paintings," he said, wondering if she could hear the strain in his voice as he pretended to study one of the watercolors with great concentration. "I'm fond of Neoimpressionists myself," he added, trying to sound a little more civilized than he felt at the moment.

Lisa followed Pete's gaze, not surprised by his remark. He struck her as a man who would appreciate all the arts, not just his own. "I probably paid too much for those pieces," she admitted, feeling a bit awkward with him. The erotic tension that had built up within her during the jam session had been defused slightly during the taxi ride home, but the memory of the charged emotions still lingered in the atmosphere like traces of musky perfume. "I bought them from an up-and-coming artist whose work I really believe in, so I figured they were a bargain at whatever price he asked." For no particular reason except nervousness, she added, "The coffee should be ready in a minute. I made it American-style—a bit less strong than what you're probably getting for your morning wake-ups at your hotel."

"My morning heart-starters, you mean," Pete said with a smile. "Back home I take coffee black, but in this country I go for café au lait, believe me. I'll enjoy a cup of American brew." Moving to another painting and peering at it, giving it such close attention he thought he needed only a monocle to look the part of a fussy art expert, Pete asked casually, "Do you know me well enough yet to tell me about your furniture-shopping affliction? My curiosity's running away with me."

Lisa perched herself on the arm of a chair, smiling quizzically. Pete really didn't forget much, she thought, amazed that he was even mildly interested in her silly quirk. "I guess I must have read too many stories as a child about homely rag dolls that no one adopted for some little girl's Christmas and lonesome tin soldiers that never got called up for active duty," she explained, then laughed. "Or, if we want to buy into my mother's theory, I identify with things that go unnoticed because I'm a typical middle child, all introspective and shy, surrounded by my more boisterous sisters and secretly wishing someone would pay more attention to me. Mom's sociology background adds a lot of depth to the studies she and Dad do, but it sometimes drives her daughters crazy. It can be difficult to grow up with a parent who understands everything you do."

"Your mother could be right about you," Pete observed. "Her theory sounds logical enough."

Lisa smiled. "That's the disturbing thing. Mom usually is right. She's very smart."

Pete liked the note of pride that invariably crept into Lisa's tone when she spoke of her family. And he held a firm belief that daughters usually turned out to be like their mothers, at least where it counted. It occurred to him that he would enjoy watching that process unfold in Lisa. "So to this day you go into a store looking for something you need and come out with something that needs you, is that it?" he asked with a burst of affection for this woman, who seemed to have by-passed all his cynical inner barriers without even trying.

"Only when it comes to furniture," Lisa said. "Of course, I have no nieces or nephews to shop for yet, so I haven't faced a shelf of dolls or a battalion of wooden warriors. I truly dread the day that happens; I don't know what I'll do."

Pete moved on to the next painting. "It's a given that you'll have an office filled with orphan dolls and dusty corporals you aren't sure would thrill the children but which you couldn't bear to leave forgotten and forlorn in the stores. But why doesn't your apartment show signs of these odd lapses of yours?"

Lisa grinned. "I stayed away from the furniture store and called in its decorator, a very intense fellow named Armand. He said things about letting my wonderful paintings set the tone, then went ahead and put it all together. I added the ritual masks and fertility figures after he'd finished, when I was sure he wouldn't see them. My Polynesian treasures mean a lot to me, but I fear they would offend poor Armand's sensibilities terribly."

Not for the first time since he'd met Lisa, Pete saw the tongue-in-cheek side of her stylishness. It was as if she knew how to play at being chic, and chose to play very well, but only on her own terms. And she didn't take the sport too seriously.

He gazed across the room at her. "You're so special, so different from anyone else I've ever met," he said quietly, adding on a sudden impulse, wanting to get the matter out of the way, "In fact, you're such an unusual woman, you haven't even asked me to explain the miserable way I acted last night. Why not, Lisa?"

"Two reasons," Lisa said, absently fluffing her hair with her fingers. "First, before I could ask you anything, I would have to explain the awful way *I* acted last night. Second, I had a chat with Harry Milton today. Not that Harry betrayed any confidences or filled me in on your life story, but when I told him about the strange clash you and I had at the villa, he did untangle a few knotted skeins for me."

"Such as?" Pete asked, covering his sudden tension by wandering over to study one last watercolor.

"Such as how I was too busy with my hang-ups to realize that you were entitled to a couple of your own," Lisa answered.

"*Your* hang-ups?" Pete said, scowling as he tried to imagine what insecurities Lisa could be harboring. Even as she spoke, she seemed so self-possessed.

Then, as an obvious thought struck him, he turned and grinned at her. "You mean your pique of jealousy?"

Lisa's lips curved in a smile. "Oh, you did notice that I wasn't too thrilled with your attentions to little Poopsie, did you?"

Pete couldn't help chuckling. "Poppy. Her name's Poppy. And it took me most of what remained of the night after I'd left you before I realized that you'd been a bit miffed. I was so busy checking out what was happening with you and the prince's good buddy . . ."

"The prince?" Lisa said, then shook her head in dismay. "So you overheard the line that awful man was trying to feed me, and still you didn't come to my rescue?"

Right up to that moment it hadn't occurred to Pete that Lisa might have wanted a rescue. He answered with just a touch of defensiveness. "Well, for all I knew, you were thrilled that he was inviting you to some ball in Monte Carlo."

Lisa rose, crossed the room, stood on tiptoe as she placed her hands on Pete's shoulders, and gently kissed his cheek. "I guess you've just hit on the crux of the matter," she said with a hesitant smile. "In our own strange, esoteric way, we've become lovers before we've learned to be friends."

Pete spanned Lisa's slender waist with his large hands. "Funny," he murmured, "once the smoke had cleared a bit on the way here, I'd started thinking that perhaps we ought to do what the old song says: Let's take it nice and easy. I said it last night, Lisa, and I meant it: I'd like to get to know you, and not just physically. For us, that'll be the simple part. The difficulty will be getting a couple of die-hard dissemblers to open up to each other outside the bedroom."

"My goodness, I've been called a lot of things," Lisa said with a laugh that betrayed a small tremor. "But never a die-hard dissembler."

"Am I right?" Pete said, his hands tightening on her waist. "Isn't there another Lisa, a secret one? Aren't there several secret ones, in fact?"

Lisa searched Pete's eyes as if looking for some kind of reassurance before she answered. Confiding in anyone, except on a superficial level, didn't come easily to her, and she knew that Pete would delve far more deeply than anyone else ever had. She wasn't sure she was ready for the kind of trust she sensed he would demand—especially when he would be moving on soon. "There probably are layers I don't choose to reveal," she answered at last. "And I have a feeling you're quite capable of stripping them away, one by one. But I need to take things slowly, which brings us to a practical matter: you're in town for perhaps nine more days, Pete. It's not enough time for anything very profound to develop between us, and I'm not very good at casual affairs. So I wouldn't blame you a bit if you decided that you came to Nice for some fun, not for soul-searching. I promise I'll understand if you want to back off right now and go find yourself another . . ." She forced a tiny grin. "Another Poopsie."

Pete laughed, but all at once a wave of intense feeling washed over him, an unfamiliar mixture of need and protectiveness. Wrapping his arms around Lisa, he pulled her hard against him. "Are you kidding?" he said huskily. "You think I'd settle for the likes of Poopsie? Why, I'll bet that girl doesn't have the faintest idea how to brew a decent cup of good old American java."

The days whizzed by for Lisa, her happiness dimmed only by the ever-present knowledge that it would end much too soon.

The night in her apartment, after the jam session, had been the watershed when the turbulent emotions she and Pete had been experiencing became more gentle, the inevitable lovemaking postponed in favor of long hours of sweet kisses and quiet, intimate talks.

As their time together whirled around them like the calendar pages in an old-fashioned movie, Lisa refused to dwell on unpleasant reality, reveling in the joy of leisurely lunches with Pete in sidewalk cafés, of leaving the office early to wander around the Cimiez grounds with him, of impulsively buying ham-and-cheese baguettes and a bottle of cold white wine and then finding a secluded spot to savor it alfresco, of musicians' parties and jam sessions and laughter-filled evenings with Harry and Sheila Milton.

Lisa began to realize that her prejudice against musicians was every bit as silly, immature, and cowardly as Justin had tried to tell her. Pete Cochrane bore no resemblance whatsoever to a sax player with wandering eyes. And if the touring demanded by his profession meant she could have only these few wonderful days with Pete, well, it was better than nothing. Lisa had made up her mind to live for the moment. Whenever she felt herself weakening, fussing about the emptiness Pete would leave behind when he'd boarded his plane for the States, she simply indulged in a session of aimless chatter with

Colette, hoping some of the girl's resilience would prove contagious. It usually did.

During her favorite times with Pete, Lisa found it unexpectedly easy to talk to him. He coaxed all sorts of stories out of her about growing up aboard the *Dreamweaver* and in the far-flung corners of the world.

For his part, Pete loved the tales of Lisa's studious but adventurous parents and her three colorful sisters, almost as if he could share vicariously in the life of such an optimistic, freewheeling family.

But he discovered that even Lisa's exciting childhood hadn't been without problems. She began opening up to him, admitting how difficult it had been for her to start caring for people only to sail literally out of their lives with no assurance of ever seeing them again. She spoke of how she'd envied Stefanie, Morgan, and Heather their more philosophical acceptance of the gypsy life—and she mentioned more than once that she wished she had her sisters' physical courage. "Some Sinclair had to be the timid one," she said lightly. "And I seemed so right for the part."

After she'd confessed hesitantly that she felt she'd lost the ability to form close attachments because she'd had to say good-bye too many times, Pete began to realize that Lisa wasn't happy to be held back by her fears. He tucked away the thought for further consideration.

"What about that fellow Justin, in New Orleans?" he asked quietly during an early evening exploration of the narrow, winding streets of Castle Hill and the old city of Nice. "You two seemed like good friends."

Lisa laughed. "I met Justin during my few settled years, the ones at college in New Orleans. He simply refused to stay behind the invisible barrier I'd tried to erect. Justin's like a big Labrador puppy; if he decides he likes you, you might as well forget about the subtle signals that tell others to back off. Unless you're prepared to swat him with a rolled-up newspaper, Justin won't notice."

Pete laughed and made a mental note of Justin's technique.

"Tell me some more about that farm in Iowa," Lisa said, turning the tables for a while. She listened in genuine fascination as Pete spoke of the pristine beauty of a green cornfield at dawn, of a sunset over a golden plain, of the rich scent of newly turned earth in spring.

"It sounds so beautiful," Lisa murmured. "Larger-than-life. How must it feel to grow up with so much sheer space all around you?"

Pete was amazed by the unexpected pride that rushed through him. "You know, you almost make me believe that my rough-hewn background is as exotic as yours," he said, giving Lisa a quick hug.

"From my point of view, your background *is* the exotic one," Lisa answered. "Mine seems rough-hewn to me. After all, I've lived with the Mud People of New Guinea!" She smiled, her eyes misting over from the fond memories. "Who are also, come to think of it, extravagantly beautiful."

Pete thought about her words for a moment, then said with a smile, "I guess it all depends on your upbringing. You know, when I first came to France, I actually felt sorry for Europeans because they didn't seem to be aware of the magic all around them. Sights that made me gasp with sheer awe were hardly noticed by the people who lived with them on an everyday basis." He laughed quietly. "Still, it never did occur to me that anyone would consider Iowa exotic." Beginning to understand just how unusual a woman Lisa was, Pete gradually found himself talking to her as he'd never talked to anyone before. He felt no need to gloss over his early determination to escape the hard life of farming.

"I guess what really bugged me," Pete said over a glass of wine in a tiny, ancient bar that had helped centuries of lovers tentatively find their way to emotional intimacy, "and still bugs me, much as I hate to admit it, is that I craved some kind of moral support from my family and got anything but." He was surprised that he could say the words aloud, that he would allow Lisa, of all people, to see the chinks in his armor. In a matter of days, he'd come a long way from the man who'd tried so hard to impress her that first night at the villa party. But Lisa made it so easy for him just to be himself. "I don't blame the folks," he went on. "They just don't think the way I do. They're fatalistic. As resigned to their niche as the peasants of a feudal system. To my parents' way of thinking, I was born the son of a poor farmer, so a poor farmer I was destined to be."

Lisa thought about how the Sinclairs unfailingly pulled for one another no matter what, how her parents had encouraged their children to reach their full potential in every way possible. She realized how much love and faith had surrounded her all her life, and it was hard for her to imagine a family being any other way. "Is it possible," she asked Pete carefully, "that your brother and your parents just didn't want to see you leave and had no idea how to tell you so except by shooting down your ambitions?"

"I'm afraid not," Pete said with a rueful smile. "My brother was visibly relieved that there would be one less person for the farm to support. And my parents just thought I was frivolous and naive. My pride would be my downfall, they said. I was trying to climb too high, so I was bound to find myself cut down to size." Pete gave his head a little shake, as if to clear it of nagging voices. "I knew from the beginning that they were wrong, but it's amazing how words like those can come back to haunt you every time you run into a roadblock," he went on, then winked at Lisa. "Or every time you find yourself surrounded by the modern-day equivalent of feudal lords and ladies in their manor houses." He laughed again, unable to talk even with Lisa about these feelings without trying to make light of them. "To this day, my father tends to ask me when I'm going to get a real job."

Lisa was a bit surprised. She'd gotten the impression that Pete had turned his back on his parents and brother. "Then you do talk to your folks?" she asked.

Pete gave her a quizzical smile and shrugged. "They're still my family," he said, as if that simple statement explained everything.

Lisa felt a tug at her heart. It was easy for her to love her parents and sisters, she realized. They were constant sources of strength and comfort. But Pete clearly loved his family without those rewards. He simply loved them.

Reaching across the dark wooden table, Lisa took Pete's hand in hers and told herself to remember this moment the next time she started thinking she was the only person with inner demons to battle. "I know now why your music is so special," she said quietly. "Why there's such a depth of emotion in your work." Aware that Pete was uncomfortable with the weighty topic, she added with a playful smile, "You wear your heart on your keyboard, Pete Cochrane. And it's a lovely heart."

Pete smiled at her. He wasn't sure how lovely his heart was, but one thing he did know: He was losing it to Lisa.

On Saturday evening, three days before Pete was scheduled to go back to the States, he told Lisa over dinner that Harry and Sheila Milton had invited them on a Sunday outing that would involve starting out very early in the morning. When Lisa fell in with his plot by accepting without asking for details, Pete said, "You don't have any phobias, do you?"

"Phobias?" Lisa asked with a puzzled frown, then gave the matter some thought. "No, I don't believe so," she said after a moment. "Unless you're planning to take me to some Côte d'Azur reptile farm for an encounter session with a distant cousin of Cuddles, I can't think of anything."

"Who's Cuddles?"

Lisa grinned. "A close friend of Morgan's. I'll tell you all about it, but for the moment, why did you ask about phobias?"

"Because Harry has booked a hot-air balloon flight," Pete answered.

Lisa blanched. "Hot-air ballooning?" She thought fast, instantly searching her mind for a way out. She hadn't thought about her private fears as phobias. "Isn't it awfully expensive?"

"I can afford it, Lisa," Pete said quietly.

Lisa picked up her glass of Perrier, then set it down, reached instead for Pete's wine, and tossed back a large gulp. She had an inspiration. "Those flights are so popular, though, we probably can't get on the one with Harry and Sheila," she said with new hope.

Pete smiled. "Harry booked for the four of us on the off chance we'd like to go. He figured it was easier to cancel than to get us included later."

"Oh," Lisa said in a small voice, then downed another swig of wine.

"I thought you had no phobias," Pete reminded her. "Would you rather not go? If you're too nervous, Lisa . . ."

"Nervous? Why would I be nervous? At Dreamweavers, we send all sorts of people ballooning. It's one of our most popular excursions, in fact." She finished off Pete's wine and held out the goblet for more.

Pete took the glass from her and set it aside. "Earning yourself a hangover is the hard way to get out of something," he chided gently. "All you have to say is no."

Lisa stared at him for several moments, holding her body very stiff. Then her shoulders sagged, and she sighed deeply. "I'm not nervous, Pete. I'm terrified. I said I was the timid Sinclair, and I wasn't exaggerating. Stefanie and Morgan are brave; they look their private terrors in the eye and wrestle them to the ground. Heather doesn't have to be brave; the fear mechanism seems to have been left out of her. She believes in fate. Nothing can happen to Heather until destiny decrees it. Or maybe she thinks the wood sprites and friendly ghosts she's forever chasing will keep her from harm. Heather's adorable, but she's a bit off-the-wall." Frowning for a moment, Lisa gave herself a little shake and returned to the main point. "I, however, studiously skirt any situation that gives me serious butterflies. I won't say I'm an out-and-out coward, but I'm definitely a . . . an avoider."

"Then there's no problem," Pete said with a smile. "We just won't go." He waited, picking at his food, pretending he considered the matter a closed issue.

Lisa chewed on her bottom lip for a while, then slammed her fist into her palm. "I'll do it."

Pete was startled. Counting on her pride, he'd anticipated her change of heart, but her assertive gesture was almost comically uncharacteristic. "Lisa, you don't have to do this," he said, wanting her to be absolutely sure. He was trying to give her an opportunity to discover that she could conquer a fear; he didn't want to force her into something she wasn't ready for. "Harry and Sheila can go on their own, and it's not important to me."

"Well, it's important to me," Lisa said. "Do you know that every single one of my sisters has gone hot-air ballooning? And when we were in Key West—that's where Morgan and Cole live—I watched from the ground while the others all took turns going up in one of those open-cockpit, World War One biplanes, complete with loop-the-loops and rolls. Lord, it was all we could do to keep Morgan from deciding to go wing-walking."

It was Pete's turn to go pale. "She wouldn't have been that foo—uh, that daring!"

With a laugh, Lisa shook her head. "We would have knocked her cold if she'd tried. Besides, Morgan's husband, Cole, seems to know how to rechannel his wife's more adventurous tendencies. But the point is, Pete, I was going on and on to you the other day about how I wished I were as courageous as my sisters. Well, you're offering me a chance to prove I can be at least a little bit brave, so I'd be the loser if I didn't accept. I'm game, Pete. I'd love to go. I intend to go. That's final." She gave him a weak smile and raised her glass of Perrier in a toast. "So we're on. As of tomorrow morning, it's up, up, and away."

Lisa stood with Pete, Harry, and Sheila in the middle of a dew-moistened plateau filled with wildflowers, breathing in the sweet perfumes and staring in suppressed horror at what looked to her like a giant wastebasket perched on the back of a pickup truck. She wondered if it was too late to change her mind.

"What a lovely name for a ballooning company," Sheila said. *"L'Aventure de l'Arc-en-Ciel,"* she read from the side of the pickup. "Rainbow Adventure. It's just perfect. I'm so excited."

Pete looked at Lisa, his brows raised questioningly. She pasted on a bright smile and hoped it would stay in place.

A tall, sandy-haired, craggy-faced man in a dark blue jumpsuit with a rainbow embroidered above the breast pocket approached them, his hand thrust out in a cheerful greeting. "I am Etienne Gabon," he said in accented English, smiling as he clasped the hand of each of his passengers. "I shall be your pilot, and Hélène is my copilot." He indicated a gamine, auburn-haired woman striding toward them with a merry smile and a bit of a swagger that would have been amusing on someone so petite had she not exuded an air of supreme confidence. "Hélène is also a certified *montgolfieriste*," Etienne said with obvious pride.

Lisa was eyeing warily the frail wicker basket that any fool could see was a death trap. Harry had said that wicker was supposed to be perfect material for the gondolas. She'd believed it—until now. And why did there seem to be so many Rainbow Adventure people lounging around the truck?

She was determined not to let her fear show. "Weren't the Montgolfier brothers the men who demonstrated ballooning at Versailles a couple of hundred years ago?" she asked, hoping no one noticed how high-pitched her voice had become. But the trivia comforted her; if people had been going up in these things for two centuries, how dangerous could the activity be? On the other hand, she thought, how many of those who'd gone up had come down in a way that had let them talk about it afterward?

Etienne beamed at Lisa's tidbit of ballooning history as if he were a teacher and she a surprisingly good student. "Now we should leave for our launching site," he said briskly. "Two of you may ride with me in the truck, two in the chase car with the crew."

"Chase car?" Lisa echoed faintly, shoving her trembling hands into the back pockets of her jeans, certain the pounding of her heart could be seen right through her chambray shirt. Chase car, she thought. It was one of those phrases like crash helmet. Not at all encouraging.

Harry and Sheila opted to ride in the car, leaving Lisa and Pete to go with Etienne. "One moment," Etienne said as they reached the truck. He went through a few motions that Lisa gathered were to test the direction of the breeze, then pointed over his shoulder and casually said, "It appears our balloon will be going that way."

"Good lord, you mean the wind's direction decides ours?" Lisa murmured, her throat constricting.

Etienne smiled. "But of course. Blasts of hot air from our burners send us upward, and we let the air cool when we wish to descend, but we do not have a great deal of control over other movements. Now if you will excuse me for a moment, I must give the crew a telephone number to call in case the chase car loses us."

A small groan escaped Lisa, but Etienne didn't seem to notice. Pete did. "Are you okay, honey?" he asked, genuinely concerned.

Lisa stared at him. He'd never used an endearment with her before. It would have turned her knees to jelly if they weren't already quivering. "I'm doing fine," she said, then laughed shakily. "Just promise one thing, will you?"

"Anything," Pete said.

Lisa gave another ragged little laugh. "If we do plummet to our doom, promise me I'll die in your arms?"

Pete gazed at her for several intense seconds, then said huskily, "You don't think I've waited this long to find you only to have it end so quickly, do you?"

The stillness was otherworldly as they floated in their rainbow-emblazoned magic balloon over the sienna-tiled rooftops, the pastel Mediterranean buildings bathed in the translucent pink light of early morning, the snowy caps of the mountains to the north veiled by a sheer mauve mist.

Lisa looked at Pete and suddenly smiled. "It's like

a casual stroll across the heavens," she said softly. "Is this the way angels feel?"

Pete reached out to trail the tip of his index finger along her delicate jawline. "I never knew it till now," he said softly.

Lisa turned her face to touch her lips to his finger. "How could I have been afraid of something so wonderful?" She tested her newfound daring by peering over the rim of the gondola, then laughed. "It's the first time I've ever looked down on flying birds."

Pete was more elated than he could remember ever being in his life, not only by the ballooning itself, but by Lisa's reaction to it. After the first few white-knuckled moments of lift-off, her fear had gradually ebbed.

As he held Lisa's hand, Pete felt a mysterious energy flowing from her into him, her skin warm against his, their pulses accelerating in perfect unison.

Searching her eyes as she smiled up at him, he saw the secret emeralds in their depths becoming larger, overtaking the soft gray, sparkling brilliantly in the early morning sun. He felt Lisa's exhilaration, and it became his own. He breathed deeply, watching the rise and fall of Lisa's breasts as she joined him in drinking great draughts of cool, sweet air.

It was happening again, Lisa thought. She and Pete were making love on a level beyond the physical. Still gazing at him, she heard herself asking their pilot, "How can the wind be carrying us anywhere, Etienne? I don't *feel* any wind." Somehow she knew the answer would be important to her.

Etienne laughed. "That is because there is no resistance. We are riding on the wind. We have become one with it."

"Imagine," she murmured. "To have become one with the wind," Lisa echoed, then brought Pete's hand to her lips. "How do we know where it'll take us? Where we'll land?" she asked with quiet excitement.

"We do *not* know," Etienne answered. "But that is part of the adventure, *oui?*"

Pete traced the outline of Lisa's full, soft mouth with his fingertip. *"Oui?"* he said in little more than a whisper.

Lisa only smiled.

Eight

Lisa and Pete floated through the remainder of their day with the Miltons in a state of dazed distraction that finally got to Harry.

"We're going to drop you two off now," he said as he drove toward Lisa's apartment after dinner in a country inn.

In the backseat of the rented Peugeot, sitting directly behind Harry, Lisa could see his grin in the rearview mirror.

"I'm getting a little tired of asking every question twice and being stared at blankly by two sets of glazed eyes," he teased.

Immediately Lisa was all apologies and denials. "Harry, this has been a wonderful day! I couldn't have asked for a better time. I must be having trouble adjusting to being earthbound again, that's all."

"And what's your excuse, Pete?" Sheila asked, her eyes sparkling as she turned to give him a knowing look.

"I guess I'm having trouble adjusting to *not* being

earthbound," he answered, smiling at Lisa and squeezing her hand. He hadn't let go of her for more than a moment throughout the whole day.

Lisa was captivated by the expression in his blue eyes, once again forgetting all about Harry and Sheila and everything else in the world except Pete's compelling magnetism. His warmth coursed through her body, fueling the electric excitement that was building to an almost unbearable intensity inside her.

". . . Become one with the wind," she remembered, knowing that at the same moment when she'd understood the wisdom of surrendering to that force of nature, she'd accepted her need for Pete as a power so vital and life-affirming, it would be self-defeating to resist.

So often, in so many ways, she'd felt that special link with Pete, that sense of joined spirits, of connected inner beings. All that remained was the physical expression of their union. The easy part, as Pete had said.

They managed a laughing good night to Harry and Sheila. "It's good to have understanding friends," Lisa said to Pete on the way up to her apartment.

"And they don't come any more understanding than Harry," Pete answered, then slid his arm around Lisa's shoulders and gave her a quick hug. "You seem to have managed to establish at least the beginnings of closeness with the Miltons, Lisa. Are they Labrador puppies like Justin, or are you putting on a good act?"

Lisa smiled, realizing that Pete was right. She'd let down her usual barriers a little, allowing a genuine affection for the other couple to take root in her. "It's not an act. I really like those people. But maybe it's because I know that when I say good-bye to them, it's not permanent. I run into Harry almost every time I'm in New Orleans, and he says he and Sheila are determined never to miss a Nice jazz festival from now on."

"So now it's time for me to score an important point," Pete said with a grin. "If people care enough, or have enough in common, no good-bye has to be permanent."

The implication of Pete's words shook Lisa. She'd isolated these few days with him from the daily reality of her life, yet he was suggesting—or at least, she *thought* he was suggesting—that his return home didn't have to mean an ending to what they'd found together.

Her hand trembled as she tried to unlock her door.

Silently Pete took the key from her, and a moment later they were stepping into Lisa's apartment. Pete closed the door behind them, shutting out the light from the hallway, leaving only the soft glow from the moon filtering through the lazily waving fronds of a palm tree outside the open window.

Drawing Lisa into his arms, Pete harnessed his emotions as he'd been doing at the end of all the previous nights when he'd left her at her door, merely touching his lips to her forehead, not daring so much as a real kiss.

But this time, he wasn't going to leave her.

Lisa felt the heat of Pete's body against hers, the throbbing duet of their hearts beat. For a moment, she was afraid she'd misunderstood his silent messages to her throughout the day, the signals of his desire. "Oh, I hope you're not kissing me good night," she murmured before she could stop herself.

Pete's arms tightened as he gazed down at her.

The moonlight in her eyes and the eager fullness of her lips cast a sensual spell over him that he knew he couldn't have denied even if he'd wanted to. And he didn't want to. "No, honey, I'm not kissing you good night. What I really hope is to be here to kiss you good morning."

"I'd like that," Lisa said, cupping her hands behind his head to draw it downward. "I'd like that so much, Pete."

"Lisa," Pete whispered, his mouth just grazing hers. "Lisa, nothing's going to end between us when I leave here. It can't. We can't let it. I won't let it." Releasing the last bonds of his restraint, he simultaneously closed his mouth over hers and swept her up in his arms, the blood racing through his veins as the eager softness of her lips ignited flames inside him that spread like a flash fire. Carrying her to the bedroom as if she were weightless, he plunged his tongue into the delicious, minted honey of her mouth.

Pete was right, Lisa told herself desperately, clinging to him as if she were drowning and only he could save her. Nothing had to end between them. Their good-bye didn't have to be permanent.

But for now, all that mattered to her was being in Pete's arms where she belonged, rejoicing in the warmth and strength of him, the demands of his mouth, the hard thrusts of his tongue.

He set her on her feet beside her bed, still appeasing his hunger with the sweet offerings of her mouth, holding her with a mixture of tenderness and possessiveness he hadn't known he could feel.

At last, raising his head, he gazed down at her again, reaching up with one hand to smooth back her hair as he marveled at what had happened in the space of a few days, at what was going to happen in the circle of moonglow that was spilling into the bedroom.

"What are you thinking?" Lisa asked softly, captivated by the play of emotions in Pete's expressive eyes and by the soothing gentleness of his touch.

"I'm memorizing," he answered, following the oval of her face with a fingertip. "This sort of moment doesn't come along every day in a person's life, you know. Fifty years from now I don't want a single second of it to be hazy in my mind. I'll want to recapture the look of you." He smiled as a fragment of a song went through his mind.

Stirred by Pete's touch as his fingers traced the outline of her mouth, Lisa felt his heat soften her body until she was molding herself to his hard masculinity, her breathing labored, her heart pounding in a primitive rhythm, her eyes closed.

He combed his fingers through the wavy strands of her hair tenderly, then learned every line of her features, even tracing the curve of her brows and the sweep of her long lashes.

He gave infinite attention to her velvety lips, the moist satin of their inner, fleshy circle. He touched the delicate curve of her ears, grazed the sensitive skin just under and behind them, then trailed downward over her throat, resting the pads of his thumbs on two hollows under her chin where her pulse leapt erratically.

Pervaded by a delicious, floating sensation, Lisa followed Pete's lead, stroking his hair, the nape of his neck, the hard line of his jaw. Her fingers toyed with the coils of hair at the open collar of his knit shirt, then moved to slide up under the shirt, her palms smoothing over his warm skin, feeling as well as hearing the sharp intake of his breath.

"Maybe I could help," he suggested, the rasp in his voice more pronounced. In one easy motion, he stripped off the shirt and tossed it aside. The expression in Lisa's eyes as she looked at him threatened to rob him of every vestige of control, and he knew he was going to have to harness all the power at his command to keep the pace as unhurried as it should be.

Lisa's gaze slowly took in Pete's muscular, lightly bronzed torso, and then her hands began moving over him, finally her lips, her tongue. With every touch and taste, she grew hungrier. She loved the textures of him, the musk-and-citrus scent, the unyielding hardness. But most of all, she loved his responses: the stiffening of his flat brown nipples when she flicked and circled them with the tip of her tongue, the gasps of excitement he couldn't seem to hold back, the tightening of his fingers as they curled around her shoulders.

Eager to feel the sensation of her skin against his, Lisa tried to undo her blouse, but her fingers fumbled at the buttons.

"Once again," Pete said, his breathing labored but his hands steady as he unfastened the buttons for her, "maybe I can help."

Pete freed her of her blouse, then held her just close enough so the tips of her breasts grazed his chest. Sighing with pleasure, Lisa curled her arms around his neck, and Pete began moving his hands in circles over her back, his touch so tantalizingly light, he sent shivers through her. Gradually his stroking grew deeper and more demanding, until he was molding her body against his and Lisa was clinging to him, tipping back her head and parting her lips.

He moved his mouth over hers, arousing her to a feverish need with his deep, erotic kisses and the intimacy of his caresses.

As Lisa felt the thrusting heat of him through the layers of denim between their bodies, she grew impatient, rotating her hips to draw Pete's attention to the barrier of cloth.

Pete hadn't needed a reminder, but he welcomed her clear, demanding signal. "Maybe this time we can both help," he said, his voice thick with desire.

Lisa nodded, then shook her head and laughed as she stepped away from Pete long enough to struggle out of her remaining clothing. "I can't believe that the first time you and I make love I have to slip gracefully out of my blue jeans," she said shakily. "I only wore them because you said I should. I almost never wear jeans, and I'd dreamed of something so much more romantic for this moment."

"Believe me, Lisa," Pete assured her with a tender smile, "my dreams of making love to you haven't focused on what you were wearing."

When they were naked, Lisa looked at Pete with such longing, he thought he would lose control completely. Spanning her waist with his two hands, he let his own gaze take in every inch of her pale, delicate body.

For the first time in her life, Lisa experienced a twinge of self-consciousness. It surprised her; she'd grown up in an atmosphere where nobody made much fuss about physical modesty. But as she stood passively under Pete's intense scrutiny, she found herself wanting to be pleasing to him, and she wasn't sure if she was.

As if sensing her anxiety, Pete feathered his hands over her breasts, then cupped the soft, gentle mounds, smiling at her. "You're even more perfect in reality than in my fantasies, Lisa. You're so lovely. Unimaginably lovely."

Lisa exulted in the sensations Pete's touch aroused in her breasts. They seemed fuller, softer, more alive than ever before, their tips engorging almost painfully.

Bending his head, Pete offered release, taking each swollen tip in turn between his lips, gently suckling, soothing, laving with his tongue.

But Lisa quickly discovered the double-edged nature of such release. As Pete's tongue swirled around one sensitive pink aureole and his lips closed around the aching nub at its center, spirals of raw, unbearably hot desire coiled through her. When he moved to start the torment anew on the other bursting tip, she gasped with pleasure and need.

Her hands moved constantly over Pete's chest, his shoulders and arms, his hard, sinewy flanks; arching her back, she thrust herself against him and rotated her hips again in another urgent, unmistakable signal. "Pete, I need you," she whispered.

He covered her breasts and throat and face with kisses, then took her mouth with a devastating, unrelenting possessiveness that told her he was about to exact her total surrender—and offer her his own.

Releasing her for a moment, Pete stood and just gazed at Lisa again, barely breathing, awed by the depth of the feelings overwhelming him. "You look so fragile," he said, wondering how he could be gentle enough not to hurt her.

"I'm not a Limoges figurine," Lisa protested with a smile. "I'm not at all fragile."

After reaching behind her to push aside the thick, flower-sprigged duvet on her bed, Pete turned to lift her in his arms, then lowered her to the soft mattress, and stretched out beside her, leaning on one elbow to smile down at her. "Perhaps you're not," he murmured, "but you're more precious than any mere Limoges. And I'll treasure you accordingly."

Lisa was moved by his words, touched by his infinite patience, and aroused by his gentle mastery as he smoothed his hands over her body, then bent to touch his lips to her throat, the mounds of her breasts, her stomach, the crease of her thighs.

Pete found his own needs taking second place to his pleasure in inflaming Lisa as he retraced his path over her body again and again, each time with a different touch, a new way to drive her to ever-greater heights of passion.

Lisa had dreamed of what Pete's hands could do to her, but her imagination hadn't come close to the reality. She responded without inhibition to the caresses of his knowing fingers, his palms, even the backs of his hands. He used his lips, his tongue, his whole body, as if he were an instrument designed specifically to delight her.

When at last Pete moved over her, Lisa was in the grip of a pent-up need, on the verge of erupting in an explosion of white heat. Her hips moved against him of their own accord, her mouth greedily captured his, her hands stroked his back, and her legs wrapped themselves around his thighs.

The more Lisa craved him, the more powerful Pete felt. Allowing just enough of his body's weight to press her into the mattress to still her demanding movements, he raised his head and breathed slowly, deeply, evenly, harnessing his control. Lisa's wondrous eyes had never looked as lovely as at this moment, all heavy-lidded with desire. Her skin was flushed, her body arching against him. He wanted the moment to last.

Poised at the entrance to her eager, moist warmth, he smiled down at her. "Lisa," he murmured, "when I'm not here with you, remember this moment. Because I will. And I'll be doing everything in my power to get back to you."

"Dear heaven, Pete," Lisa whispered, "I'll remember this moment for the rest of my life."

Finally plunging into her, Pete held her gaze and saw a film of tears cloud her huge, gray-green eyes. He lay still for a moment to give her body time to adjust, but Lisa's legs clasped him and urged him on. He began to move, holding her, establishing a rhythm she caught as easily as if she were part of him.

Their pace quickened sooner than Pete wanted it to; he wished their first fusion could last forever. But he'd controlled his passion for too long already, and Lisa's soft surrender carried him to irresistible peaks of excitement and fulfillment.

Lisa felt what was happening to Pete. Their bodies were so attuned, she knew when he'd joined her in climbing the highest summit, and just as he reached the very edge of the precipice, the heat of him inside her triggered an eruption that catapulted them into a free flight.

Pete held Lisa with fierce tenderness during their slow descent, the pulsations of their joined bodies gradually subsiding. At last, he moved to lie beside her, nestling her in the cradle of his arms. "There's something you should understand," he said after a long while, absently stroking her arm.

Lisa braced herself, already hurting before he said another word. Was he going to retract his promise to come back? Now that the pressure of frustrated desire had been relieved, was he about to see things more realistically? Was he . . . ?

She put on the brakes right there. Because she'd surrendered so completely to Pete, she was feeling vulnerable, she told herself. It was a perfectly understandable reaction. But feeling vulnerable was no excuse for lapsing into fears and suspicions that didn't belong in any bed she shared with Pete Cochrane—or in any moment she shared with him. "What should I understand?" she asked, cuddling even closer to him.

To Lisa's surprise, Pete laced his fingers through her hair and gently tugged, tilting back her head so she was looking up at him. "Just this," he said with feigned menace. "Don't forget: I will be coming back to you. And I wouldn't take kindly to finding out that my lady had gone to some ball in Monte Carlo with another guy, prince or no prince."

Lisa's heart skipped a beat. She felt herself melting again, wanting Pete, thrilled by his possessiveness. "Well, let me tell you something, Pete Cochrane," she said in a soft, loving threat of her own. "Beware of Poopsies and redheads who fall out of their dresses, because if you don't, I'll know. Don't ask how I'll know. I just will. And I'll punish you the Bora Bora way."

Pete's mouth twitched. He loved Lisa's feline streak. He wanted to see more of it. "What's the Bora Bora way?" he asked.

Lisa had no idea. But if there was one thing she'd picked up from her wager-loving oldest sister, it was how to bluff. "Pete," she said as she sat up and looked down at him, curling her fingers around his wrists and pinioning his arms to the bed as if he were her helpless prisoner. "Pete," she said again in a hushed voice as she suddenly straddled him, "you don't ever want to know."

• • •

With no consideration for fragile beginnings, time simply ran out. All of a sudden, Pete was gone, and Lisa was alone.

She was stunned by the intensity of her pain as she sat on the low stone wall of the Promenade des Anglais, watching a jet rising from the airport across the bay.

Remembering the times she and Pete had strolled along the walkway, Lisa closed her eyes for a moment, trying to recapture his presence, as if somehow he'd left traces of it there for her to draw on.

He hadn't let her take him to the airport. "There'll be no tragic, brave farewell scene for us," he'd said just before leaving her apartment. "I'll play my club dates and get the meetings about my new album out of the way, and then I'll take some time to come here to concentrate on composing—and on you. I wish I could say exactly when I can make it back, honey, but you'll see me again. Soon."

"I'll keep a light on," she'd promised.

Watching the jet until it was a tiny silver shard in the distant sky, Lisa felt physically ill.

Old habits came back in a rush. She deserved to be this miserable, she began thinking. Hadn't she known better than to get involved with Pete? Hadn't she experienced enough good-byes in her life to know they were inevitable? Hadn't she learned by the time she'd reached adolescence that anyone who got too close to her left a terrible void when the time came for another parting?

"Oh, don't be such a dope," she muttered aloud. Pete had said he'd be back. What was she doing? Where was her faith? How could she allow those insistent, pushy fears to keep dragging her down?

"Now cut the self-pity," she scolded herself. "Believe the man."

A baby poodle trailing a rhinestone-studded leash scampered up to her, tilted its head to one side, and gave her a quizzical stare, as if asking whether she always talked to herself.

"Hi there," she said, extending her hand slowly, palm-up, so the puppy wouldn't feel threatened. "You're in big trouble," she warned as she saw a red-faced man in a too-tight jogging outfit come puffing along the promenade. Afraid the poodle's master was flirting with a heart attack, Lisa picked up the end of the leash and waved it to show that she had things under control.

The pup spared a cavalier glance backward when it heard "Piaf!" shouted in a desperate squeak.

"Piaf," Lisa repeated with a laugh. The ridiculous little ball of fluff wagged its tail, involving its entire hind end in the gesture. She could have sworn the animal smiled back at her. "Well, Piaf, you won't catch me singing torch songs and crying into my cognac," Lisa said firmly. "My Pete is coming back, and that's that. As your namesake would say, little Piaf, '*Je ne regrette rien.*' "

The dog cocked its head to the other side, apparently aware that Lisa was whistling in the dark. As Piaf's master finally caught up, thanked Lisa profusely, and dragged the poodle away, it gazed soulfully back at her.

"I know how you feel," Lisa murmured. "That's about how I looked when Pete left."

Only after she'd waved good-bye to her new little friend did she realize she'd just had an intimate chat with a dog. In public.

Falling in love was enough to make a person slightly

eccentric, she thought, getting to her feet as she decided that a retreat from that particular section of the promenade was in order. People were giving her peculiar looks and knowing smiles. The best therapy was work, she decided, heading in the direction of her office.

She was halfway there before the realization hit her: She *was* in love with Pete. But was it possible, after knowing the man for less than two weeks?

Yes, she thought. It was more than possible. It was a reality. She was in love. And she'd known Pete much, much longer than the few precious days of the jazz festival. She'd known him forever.

A week passed, then two, then three. Lisa kept the faith. Pete helped with regular calls and funny postcards from wherever his gigs took him.

Excitedly he told her over the phone about the deal that was in the works for his second album. "It looks as if the money men are prepared to dig deep," he said. "They're talking real advertising dollars, for a change."

Lisa was pleased for him. Thrilled for him, in fact. But she missed him more every day.

She continued to see Harry and Sheila until their holiday ended and they, too, had to go home. Lisa was sad to see them leave, but she realized that good-byes no longer had the power to devastate her. She was shedding the emotional fetters of the little girl who'd learned over the years to be afraid of closeness. She was learning to be more like Morgan, to embrace life as it came, to give of herself without asking for guarantees.

She began making changes at work that she'd

been considering for months, hiring an extra staff member to start training to replace Marie Leblanc, her top tour guide. Ultimately she wanted Marie to take over the day-to-day management of the office.

And when Colette started making noises about wanting to try her hand at leading a few tour groups, Lisa happily arranged for temporary receptionists twice a week so Colette could go out in the field. Lisa had thought for some time that Colette had outgrown her present duties.

"You wouldn't be planning to leave us and run off with your musician, would you?" Colette asked teasingly as she stood in Lisa's office filing travel manifests.

Lisa wasn't prepared to admit, even to herself, that Pete had anything to do with her plans to make the Nice operation of Dreamweavers self-sufficient. It had been her goal from the first day she'd opened the office. "Now that all our systems and tours are in place," she said truthfully—but not quite honestly—"it's time I got more involved in the marketing end of things, which would mean going back to the States more often. After all, most of our clients are Americans, and I can't keep depending on Stefanie to do the major presentations I should be handling."

Colette smiled wisely and went back to her desk.

Three weeks passed, which Lisa knew wasn't a terribly long time—but it felt like an eternity. And though Pete couldn't say when he'd be back in Nice, Lisa's faith didn't waver.

It just wobbled a little from time to time.

Nine

Pete arrived back in Nice five weeks after he'd left.

Lisa thought her heart would burst when she saw him get off the plane, and as he dragged her into his arms and buried his face in her hair, murmuring her name over and over, she felt as if she were breathing properly for the first time since he'd gone.

They spent an entire, glorious month together, their days filled with picnics in the monastery gardens overlooking the Cimiez ruins, with Sunday explorations of the villages that were tucked into coves all along the Azure Coast, with meals cooked in Lisa's kitchen after a lively session of bargaining at the farmers' market. And their nights were rich with passionate, bonding love.

"It seems foolish now that you rented your little villa," Lisa said as she and Pete cuddled in her bed on the last Sunday of their precious month, exactly a week before he was scheduled to leave. "You haven't spent a single night in it, and you could have set up that electronic keyboard of yours here."

"True," Pete said, kissing the top of Lisa's head, hating the prospect of the mornings ahead when he would be waking up without her. "But when I first came back to Nice, we needed that villa. It would have been premature for me to have moved in with you officially at that point." He laughed and hugged her closer. "This way, things just evolved."

"And so beautifully," Lisa said, touching her lips to his chest, her voice dropping to a husky murmur. "I do love the things that evolve between us."

She didn't dread the coming separation as much as she had the first one. Her doubts had been put to rest when Pete had returned just as he'd promised he would. Besides, her own plans were progressing nicely.

The gradual changing of the guard at Dream-weavers was working even better than she'd expected: Marie was as talented a manager as a tour leader, Colette was blossoming into a guide with her own special flair, and the new staff members were settling comfortably into their own niches.

Lisa had several valid reasons for visiting the States soon; all she needed was a little encouragement from Pete.

When that encouragement wasn't forthcoming, she took a deep breath, beat back her tendency to keep her self-doubts a secret, and placed a call to New Orleans. "Steffie, I need advice," she said, then spilled out her feelings about Pete. "I'm sure he cares for me," she said after she'd bared her soul. "But why isn't he asking whether I could go back to the States with him, or meet him there later?

Stefanie didn't hesitate. "If you were Pete, would

you ask someone who's in business to drop everything and fly across the Atlantic to be with him
whenever he happens to have time to spare from his
own tight schedule?" she asked in the no-nonsense
voice that Lisa loved. "On the other hand, I'll bet you
a lunch at Antoine's that Pete would be thrilled if he
thought you had your own reasons to be over here."

Lisa smiled, her spirits lifting. "You know something, Steffie? You're a lot smarter than everybody
says."

Stefanie laughed. "I knew the truth would come out
eventually, squirt. And by the way—whether or not you
come over because of Pete, I really would appreciate
it if you could see your way clear to handling the
presentation in Chicago. Those gallery owners I've
been telling you about are planning a top-of-the-line,
major art tour throughout France for a sizable group.
This is one pitch that needs Lisa Sinclair in person."

"I'll be there," Lisa said happily. One of Pete's
upcoming club dates would be in Chicago. She told
herself that Stefanie was right, that Pete would be
thrilled when she told him she could meet him there.

The days, as one of Pete's favorite songs said,
dwindled down to a precious few.

For the past month, he'd felt his creative juices
flowing as never before. Like so many artists of
various disciplines, he was inspired by the sheer sensuality of the Riviera and Provence: the clear Mediterranean light; the brilliant colors of sunflower fields,
of pine and cypress forests, of crystal waterfalls
splashing into hidden ravines; the fragrances of wild
lavender, citrus, jasmine, and roses; the constant,
throbbing pulse of the sea.

The popularity he was experiencing in Nice didn't hurt either. He was certain he would never forget the thrill he'd gotten the first time he'd heard his album being played on a portable radio on the Promenade des Anglais. His confidence had begun to soar, and with it, his compositions.

Most of all, Pete was inspired by Lisa. She was his muse in the best and fullest sense, her warmth and acceptance and belief helping to release an untapped energy within him. But the thought of another long separation from her was like a storm cloud lurking behind the ever-present Côte d'Azur sun.

He started thinking seriously about the future.

Lisa decided to make Pete's last night in Nice special—and to set the scene for what would be, for her, an act of unprecedented boldness.

"I'll take care of everything," she said when Pete called her at her office. "We like picnics; I'm going to try to create the pièce de résistance of picnics."

"But you're working all day," he protested. "Let me just pick up something."

"I've already organized the whole thing, including the wine," Lisa said firmly. "I've known for two weeks that Marie was scheduled to have her wisdom tooth out today, poor girl, so I've been very efficient. I won't get out of the office until about four, but I can still be ready and waiting for you at my apartment, Red Riding Hood basket in hand, at six o'clock."

"Six it is," Pete said. By this time, he knew there was no point arguing with Lisa when she'd made a decision.

He called her back at three. "Have you peeked outside lately?"

"Yes, and I can't believe it!" Lisa answered. "How could it rain on our picnic? And the day started out looking so sunny!"

"You sound like a disappointed little kid," Pete said with a laugh that was slightly forced. He was trying not to give in to the ridiculous superstition that the rain was some kind of bad omen. "We'll just think of something else to do, that's all."

"No, we won't," Lisa insisted. "We'll have our picnic as scheduled. I have no intention of wasting all the effort I've already put into it—or all that food."

"What if it's still raining when I come to pick you up?"

"Rainy picnics can be the very best kind," Lisa said, determined that not even a downpour would dampen her spirits. "We used to have some of the most wonderful picnics on the *Dreamweaver* when there was nothing else to do but pull into some cove to wait out a storm," she added cheerfully. When she'd begun seeing Pete, she reminded herself, she'd known the problems; she couldn't be a baby about the separations now. And there was the prospect of Chicago—assuming Pete really would want her there. "So I'll see you at six?" she asked, squelching a nagging doubt.

Pete chuckled. "Six o'clock sharp, honey. Rain or shine."

There was still a drizzle when Pete arrived at Lisa's apartment promptly at six.

He smiled as he knocked, wondering what her alternate plan for their picnic was.

When Lisa opened the door, Pete caught his breath, stunned by the impact of her loveliness.

He'd expected to see her in one of her stylishly casual outfits—perhaps the white cotton playsuit with the halter top that gave her a Harlow look, or the gauzy, off-the-shoulder peasant dress Morgan had sent her from Nassau. Whatever Lisa chose to wear, she always managed to be pretty and chic and exciting.

But this time, he thought as he just stood there staring at her, she was magnificent. If someone told him she was a princess from a mysterious, exotic land, he'd have had no trouble believing it.

Never had she looked more regal yet more provocative than in the ice-blue creation that skimmed loosely over her slender form, the material an opaque but tissue-thin silk intricately embroidered in silver thread around the neckline and at the hem of the flowing sleeves, tiny silk buttons all the way down the front, delicate silver sandals on her feet.

Pete had to clear his throat before he could speak, and even then, his voice was hoarse. "I'll never get used to all the different ways you manage to look exquisite, Lisa. Tonight you're like . . . like a sapphire."

Thrilled with Pete's reaction to her efforts to be especially pleasing to him, Lisa smiled, reached for his two hands, and gently tugged him in from the hallway, stretching up on tiptoe to kiss his cheek as she pushed the door shut behind him.

Her perfume was different, Pete thought; not the subtle fragrance she usually wore, but something bolder, richer, unabashedly seductive. It had its desired effect on his senses. He cleared his throat again. "I didn't realize we were having a formal picnic," he said with an attempt at a laugh. "Maybe I should go back to my place and change from these jeans into my tux."

"You look wonderful, Pete. You always do. And what I'm wearing isn't formal. It's my own version of a galabia, the loose robes Arabs wear." Lisa lowered her voice confidentially. "I'm about to tell you one of the darkest of my secrets: I don't pay designer prices for my clothes. I have a genius of a dressmaker who can copy any picture I show her or even draw for her, as long as I can come up with the right fabric. She made this galabia for me a year ago, but I've never worn it. I was waiting for a very special occasion. And this afternoon, when I decided that the special occasion had arrived, I stopped at a little store that specializes in such things and picked up a galabia for you. It's far more masculine than this one, you'll be glad to know." She turned and waved her hand toward the center of the living room. "You see? We're going to have our picnic right here." With a deliberately wicked smile, she added huskily, "So why don't you go into the bedroom and slip into something comfortable while I peel you a grape?"

Pete tore his gaze from Lisa and scanned the make-shift picnic grounds, smiling and shaking his head in wonder as he saw that in the middle of the carpet she had put down a white linen tablecloth and had piled cushions on either side of it. A bottle of champagne was nestled in a silver ice bucket, candles of every shape and size flickered throughout the darkened room, and there really was a fruit tray laden with bunches of grapes as well as ripe peaches, plums, and nectarines.

Tantalizing aromas from the kitchen, the *Arabian Nights* ambience, and Lisa's ethereal loveliness made such a heady assault on Pete's senses, he almost decided on the spot to scrap his plans for going back to the States, make the most of his career success in France, and simply announce he wanted to stay with her.

But he couldn't. What he felt for Lisa, what he wanted to achieve, what he needed to become for his own sake—and now for hers, as well—would keep driving him no matter what the temptation. He had to grab for the success that would prove to himself and everyone else that he hadn't been crazy to carve out a career in music, the success that would make him feel equal to anyone in Lisa's Côte d'Azur set, the success that finally seemed to be within reach.

For tonight, though, nothing mattered to him but Lisa. "I'll go change," he said quietly, heading for the bedroom to give himself a further pep talk on his long-range goals and to put on Lisa's gift.

The galabia was a loose robe in dark blue Egyptian cotton, satiny smooth against his naked skin, cool and comfortable.

Lisa, as thoughtful as ever, had provided sandals for him. Pete smiled, his pulse quickening as he wondered just how detailed her plans for the evening were.

Lisa's idea of a picnic, he discovered soon after he'd returned to the living room, was his idea of a sultan's feast: stuffed vine leaves, tomato and feta cheese salad, triangles of pita bread with a tangy chick-pea puree dip, savory couscous, miniature meat kebabs with apricot sauce, grilled prawns, lemon-and-basil chicken breasts, and for dessert, baked figs in wine served warm, with a wedge of raisin-studded cream cheese.

Much later, Pete sighed, replete with delicious food and excellent champagne—and pervaded by an ever-intensifying desire for Lisa. "Did we just have Italian, North African, Spanish, Greek, or French cuisine?" he asked.

"All of the above," Lisa answered, picking up a bunch of grapes. "The dishes we had were just . . . Mediterranean, I suppose."

"It was fantastic," Pete said, lying back against a pile of pillows. He smiled as he saw that Lisa was, in fact, gracefully peeling a grape.

She moved from her place on the opposite side of the tablecloth to recline beside him, teasingly stroking his lips with the sweet flesh of the ripe offering until he drew it slowly into his mouth and then licked the juices from her fingertips.

Lisa felt the familiar unfurling of countless, tiny coils of heat within her, radiating into every part of her body. Languidly she prepared another succulent morsel, held it between her rounded lips, and cradled Pete's face between her palms as she shared the luscious fruit with him.

Outside, the palm tree swished its wet leaves against the shuttered window and the rain drummed lightly on the thirsty grass below.

As if there were no limit on their time together, Pete and Lisa slowly worked open the buttons of each other's robes while indulging in teasing love play, and then lay naked in the candlelight, every object in the room fading into the background except the primitive masks and burnished icons of the South Pacific.

In the setting that magically transported her to a world devoid of pretense, Lisa shed the last of her inhibitions, giving herself to Pete with unrestrained abandon and utter trust.

An atavistic power within Pete suddenly slipped its leash, his primal need to conquer released by the demands of Lisa's fierce, total surrender. He took her as if staking out his territory; she received him as if claiming what belonged to her. There was nothing gentle about their loving. Stripped of the thin veneer of civilization, they exploded together again and again until at last they lay exhausted in each other's arms.

After a long while, Lisa surprised Pete by rolling away from him and laughing softly, stretching like a contented tigress. "I'd planned this evening so carefully," she said as she reached out to hold Pete's hand. "But we deviated from the script."

"Isn't improvisation terrific?" Pete said, smiling at her. "But what was supposed to happen?"

Lisa turned on her side and propped herself up on one elbow, absently walking two fingers up Pete's torso, as if counting his ribs. "Well, I'd meant for our after-dinner grape-peeling to extend to coffee and brandy, because there was something I wanted to talk to you about. Somehow, I forgot. But would you like coffee now? Cognac?"

Pete smiled. "I only want you, Lisa. Stay close to me."

Encouraged by his request, Lisa decided to say what she had on her mind and hope for the best. "On the subject of my staying close to you . . ." She took a deep breath. Risking rejection didn't come easily to her. "I have to go to the States soon. Maybe you and I could match schedules and get together there."

Pete stared up at her, hardly believing his ears. "Why wouldn't you have mentioned this possibility until now?" he asked quietly.

A tiny fear took root in Lisa. "I . . . I wasn't sure you'd . . ." Once again, she had to pause to take a deep breath. It was amazing how quickly her confidence was slipping away. "I was hoping you'd suggest that I join you over there," she said, forcing herself to speak firmly. "When you didn't, I decided to try being assertive and bring up the possibility myself. But look, if it wouldn't work out, Pete, if you'll be too busy, or—"

"Wouldn't work out? Too busy?" he said, aghast as he saw Lisa's lightning-fast retreat. Reaching for her, he dragged her into his arms and felt the stiffness in her body that he thought had disappeared forever. "Honey, I've been so miserable about leaving you," he said, stroking her hair with one hand, her back with the other. "It would have made the past few days so much easier if I'd known there was even a chance you might be able to take some time off to be with me. I wanted to ask you, but how could I?"

Lisa buried her face in his shoulder. "That's what Steffie told me," she murmured.

"Remind me to thank Stefanie when I meet her," Pete said, wrapping his arms around Lisa to hold her even closer. "Now, about our schedules: I'm not booked into New Orleans for this trip, but I'm sure I could manage to get there. My gigs this time are only Wednesday-to-Saturday stints, so I'd be able to fly down to meet you."

"You wouldn't need to," Lisa said. "I'll be in New Orleans for only a couple of days, and then I have to go to Chicago. You do have a club date there, don't you?"

Pete willed himself not to react. But he groaned inwardly. Why Chicago? Why not New York or Detroit? "I'll be in the Windy City for two weeks, starting the week after next," he answered lightly, continuing to hold Lisa, feeling guilty on several counts because having her with him in Chicago might mean a complication he wasn't ready for. But he couldn't hurt her by letting on that there was even the slightest difficulty. "Could you spend the whole two weeks with me, or would that be hoping for too much?" he asked.

Lisa wondered if she'd heard a slight strain in Pete's voice, felt a sudden tension in his body. But she told herself she was being oversensitive. He was pleased that she could join him in Chicago. She was certain of it. After all, wasn't he asking her to stay with him for two full weeks? "I think I could manage," she said, snuggling against him.

Pete lay with her in his arms, listening to the rain, all at once not very proud of himself.

Lisa's first impression when she ran into Pete's arms at O'Hare Airport was that he looked more tired than she'd ever seen him.

"I've missed you, honey," he whispered, his lips against her ear as he held her with fierce desperation. "I love you, Lisa," he heard himself saying before he could hold back the words. "I love you so damn much."

She tipped back her head and stared at him.

Pete laughed with a shock that was at least as great as Lisa's. He'd had no intention of saying those words. Especially not when so many things were falling apart. "Now I know how you felt that first night when we made love, and you said you'd imagined wearing something more romantic than jeans. I certainly had imagined a more romantic setting than an airport for the first time I told you how I feel about you."

Lisa smiled, her eyes misty. "To paraphrase the

answer you gave me, when I've dreamed of hearing those words from you, I haven't been paying much attention to the backdrop."

It took a moment for Pete to grasp the real essence of what Lisa was telling him. If she'd been dreaming of hearing those words, he thought, she must have wanted to say them. He captured her mouth in a kiss that spoke more than all the words in the world. Then, releasing her, he smiled and waited, his heart pounding.

Lisa didn't make him wait long. "I love you, Pete. You know I do. You've known it for weeks. And I've wanted to say it, but I . . . I don't know, I just . . ."

"Don't tell me," he interposed with a laugh, hugging her. "You held back because you were afraid you might impose a sense of obligation on me. And because the independent feline in you required that I confess my feelings first." Chuckling, he hugged her again. "And most of all, because you're a Sinclair."

Lisa nuzzled into his warm embrace. "What does my being a Sinclair have to do with it?"

"I don't know, but instinct tells me that your being a Sinclair has everything to do with everything," Pete answered. "Now, I've gotten us a great hotel suite overlooking Lake Michigan, the champagne's on ice, and we have some celebrating to do."

"The album?" Lisa asked as they waited for a taxi. "Is it going well, then?"

Pete's expression clouded. "No, I just meant a celebration of being together again."

"You've run into a hitch," Lisa stated. She'd sensed from her most recent telephone conversations with Pete that something was wrong.

"Let's just say I have to make a tough decision," Pete answered as the taxi pulled up.

Lisa found Pete's words, his whole manner, slightly ominous. She had to keep reminding herself that he'd just said he loved her.

"What's the tough decision?" Lisa asked as she and Pete stood at the hotel suite's large picture window and looked out at Lake Michigan. "Or is it something you prefer not to talk about?"

Pete grinned at her over the rim of his champagne flute. "That's my honey," he said, raising the glass to her in a toast. "Straight to the point, huh?"

"I can't help it," Lisa said. "You seem so strained, Pete. Are you sure I'm not going to be . . . well, in your way?"

"About as much as my right hand is in my way," he answered, then went to get the champagne bottle to top up their half-full glasses.

Lisa waited, sensing that Pete was using the moment to collect his thoughts. She hoped she wasn't going to have to be brave about something in the next few minutes.

"First, about the album," he said as he filled the glasses. "There is a small hitch. Maybe a big hitch. It seems that if I sign on with the guys who are ready to sink a lot of money into promotion, I have to do things their way, hire the studio musicians they provide instead of using the people I feel are best—and fill most of the album with what would most charitably be described as easy listening tunes."

Lisa nodded. "And the offer is tempting because once you've established a name, and perhaps hit it big financially with a well-promoted album, you might have some clout and then be able to do things your way."

"Exactly," Pete said, returning the champagne bottle to the ice bucket. He stood looking down into his glass rather than at Lisa. "Then there's this other little studio—a low-budget, seat-of-the-pants operation. These people want to produce a Pete Cochrane album, not a collection designed to be played in supermarkets to lull shoppers into buying the expensive junk food in the middle aisles."

"Whew," Lisa murmured. "I hope you're not asking my opinion, because I wouldn't know what to say." The truth was, she knew what she hoped Pete would decide, but she didn't feel she had the right to speak up.

"I wouldn't put that kind of responsibility on you," Pete said, meeting her eyes and smiling at her, not surprised by her reaction. But he wondered: Would Lisa prefer a musician with artistic integrity, or one who'd hit the big time? "This is a decision I'm going to have to make for myself," he said, then added, "Like another one I made just before you arrived."

Lisa's fingers tightened around the stem of her glass. "My goodness, you've been very . . . decisive," she said with a forced smile. For some reason, she couldn't stop being braced for trouble.

"I mentioned to you that my weekdays here are just Wednesday to Saturday, didn't I?" Pete asked.

"Yes, you did mention that," Lisa said warily. Was he going to tell her he had to go somewhere else on the other days? Somewhere she couldn't follow?

"Yes, I did mention it," Pete said absently, raking his fingers through his hair and beginning to pace the room.

"Pete, you're making me very nervous," Lisa finally said. "If you have something unpleasant to tell me, please get it over with."

He stopped in his tracks and met her level gaze. "It's my folks."

Lisa paled. "Oh, Pete, has something happened?"

"No, no, nothing like that," Pete said hastily, then felt silly about being so melodramatic about what was on his mind. "It's just that my mother's birthday is next week, and my folks know I'm here in Chicago, so they would wonder if I didn't go to see them. Originally I'd planned to head over there next Sunday." He began pacing again.

Lisa waited, her nerves taut. The logical thing for Pete to do, it seemed to her, was to ask her to go to Iowa with him. He'd said he loved her. Wouldn't a man want the woman he loved to meet his family? To have his family meet her?

"Honey," Pete said at last, "for some time now I've known that you and my folks would have to meet sooner or later, but I just kept thinking—and, admittedly, hoping—it would happen later rather than sooner."

Lisa's tension ebbed just a little. For a wild moment, she'd begun to wonder whether Pete had been about to announce he had a wife and ten children on that Iowa farm.

Realizing that her fears about musicians and their tendency to juggle multiple lives hadn't quite been put to rest, and that Pete still had a few vulnerabilities of his own to deal with, Lisa tried to make light of the situation. "What's the problem? Either you go to Iowa while I stay here, or I go to Iowa with you," she said matter-of-factly, then suppressed a grin. "Of course, if you choose to leave me behind, I'll be so distraught, I'll probably run off with Dave Brubeck's drummer."

Pete stared at her for several tense moments, then

laughed, shaking his head. "Lisa honey, you just showed me that there's no problem at all. You know, I went through days of soul-searching before I finally decided to ask you to go to Iowa with me. My folks are stereotypical Midwesterners—tactiturn and blunt, a bit suspicious of outsiders, meaning anyone born beyond the borders of their county. You'll be the first girl I've taken home to meet them, and I was concerned that their rough-around-the-edges ways might bother you. It took me a while to get it through this thick skull of mine that my hesitation was an insult to you as well as to them. And what you've just made me realize is that it could be a lot of fun seeing what happens when the Bora Bora baby meets American Gothic."

Lisa put down her glass, walked over to Pete, took his glass and set it on a nearby table, and twined her arms around his neck. "Pete Cochrane," she said with a relieved, happy smile, "I would be honored and thrilled to meet the people who managed to turn out a man like you. And don't you worry," she added. "I've lived with reformed cannibals and headhunters; how daunting can an Iowa farmer be?"

"That, my love, is exactly what has me worried," Pete said with a grin that was only half-teasing. He swept Lisa up in his arms and carried her to the king-size bed, deciding that they'd done enough talking for a while.

Ten

When the moment for the Iowa visit actually arrived, Pete couldn't help being edgy. He told himself it didn't matter how things went, but the hard truth was that he wanted his family to like Lisa, to see her for what she was and not be prejudiced because she was stylish and cultivated and a success at her own career. Reverse snobbishness, he thought. He'd come by it honestly.

The question of whether Lisa would like his family crossed his mind as well, but he had a lot more faith in her tolerance than in the open-mindedness of the Cochranes.

His brother and sister-in-law were waiting in the arrivals area of the Des Moines airport.

"It's easy to see that you and Ted are brothers," Lisa whispered to Pete when she saw the tall, lean man with the same dark hair and brows and strong features that made Pete so gorgeous. With a mischievous smile, she added, "He's a hunk too."

Though Pete was pleased by Lisa's words, his territorialism flared, albeit playfully. "And Ted has been nuts about his sweet little brown-haired Addie ever since he first tugged on her ringlets about twenty-five years ago."

"You can tell from the way he's standing there with his arm around her," Lisa said softly, suddenly aware that Pete's arm was around her own shoulders in exactly the same way.

After hugging the diminutive and obviously pregnant Addie, and shaking hands with Ted, Pete proudly but somewhat nervously made introductions.

Noticing that Addie's glance skimmed approvingly over Lisa, without the kind of shrinking withdrawal he'd seen his sister-in-law suffer around other women she'd thought of as glamorous, Pete realized how much care Lisa had given to choosing her outfit. She had too much integrity to play down her stylishness, but Pete knew it was no accident that her gray flannel trousers, red wool bomber-style jacket, cream-colored Shetland sweater, and classic loafers looked terrific without being showy.

But it was during the drive to the farm that Pete began to appreciate Lisa fully.

Once he'd learned from his laconic brother that the year had been a pretty good one—which meant there hadn't been more than three natural but survivable disasters—and once the shy Addie had unnecessarily acknowledged that yes, their first baby was due very soon, Pete had braced himself for the usual awkward gaps in the conversation.

But for a change there weren't any, and Pete began to realize that Lisa was the catalyst who was managing to get both Ted and Addie talking, to the point where they were actually chatty.

Lisa's technique was time-honored but effective.

She simply asked questions—intelligent ones that required responses of more than a word or two—and then she really listened to the answers.

By the time the station wagon pulled into the long driveway of the Cochrane homestead, Pete was surprised to learn there was quite a bit he hadn't known about the problems and rewards involved in operating a farm these days. Things had changed since his chore-doing years, and it occurred to him that his longtime defensiveness toward his family had made him just as oblivious of their problems and dreams as he'd felt they'd been to his. It was quite a revelation.

"Nice eyes," Pete's father said while Addie was showing Lisa upstairs to the guest room.

Pete was deeply pleased. From Hank Cochrane, those two words were extravagant praise. Obviously Lisa had made a big hit with the man.

When Pete had a moment alone with Lisa, he said quietly, "I'm sorry about this separate rooms thing. My parents are pretty old-fashioned."

"It's their home, so we follow their rules," Lisa said with a smile. "And it's a wonderful home, by the way. It's exactly what I'd pictured a Midwest farmhouse would look like."

Seeing the place as if for the first time, Pete wondered if it really was much more pleasant than he'd remembered it. "Have you been doing some redecorating?" he asked his mother, noting that Lisa was pitching in to set the big kitchen table for supper, and that her help, to Pete's amazement, was being accepted. Peggy Cochrane rarely allowed anyone besides Addie to lift a finger in her domain.

But Lisa's casual insistence on doing what she cheerfully referred to as her share seemed to have disarmed his mother. "Redecorating?" she repeated, showing Lisa where to find the cutlery before glancing at Pete. "It's just a bit of painting and wallpapering," she added with a hint of a smile, pushing back a strand of hair that had escaped the elastic band holding back her rich, dark mane.

For just an instant, Pete saw a glimpse of the twenty-year-old college girl who'd fallen for a tall, good-looking country boy and had married him even after she'd found out she wouldn't have an easy existence as a farmer's wife.

As Addie handed him a stack of plates, pleasantly suggesting that if he insisted on getting in the way he might as well make himself useful, Pete found himself wondering whether he would have the nerve to ask Lisa to walk away from whatever life she'd planned, just to throw her lot in with his.

Times—and people—had changed over the past couple of decades, he reminded himself. Unless he did manage to grab the brass ring that was so close, yet so elusive, he wasn't even sure he would feel he had the right to ask Lisa to work out compromises in her career to be with him.

"Lisa, that pendant you're wearing keeps catching my eye," Peggy Cochrane said as everyone sat around the kitchen table well into the wee hours—which meant, in his parents' household, until after nine o'clock. "Is it ivory?"

"It's a shell," Lisa answered, holding up the intricate bit of filigree. "It's scrimshaw, a kind of carving that's done on whalebone and ivory and seashells. A

Tahitian friend of mine made this for me as a going-away gift when my parents accepted a writing assignment that took us to New Zealand. It's pretty, isn't it?"

"Beautiful," Peggy said. "I don't think I've ever seen anything so dainty."

On impulse, Lisa reached behind her neck to undo the clasp of the gold chain, then handed the necklace to Pete's mother. "Please accept it as a gift from me for your hospitality," she said with a smile.

Pete sat very still. His parents were overly proud and easily offended. He knew Lisa's offer had been made out of simple generosity, but his folks had no way of understanding that Lisa cared little for possessions, that she truly took more pleasure from giving things away to appreciative people than from owning them.

His mother tilted her head to one side and gave Lisa a quizzical look. "Why would you give me your necklace? It must mean a lot to you," she said with a hint of suspicion. "And wouldn't your friend, the one who carved this shell, wouldn't he be hurt if he knew you'd given it away?"

Lisa smiled. "Actually, it's a she, and she'd be very proud. Besides, the shell itself isn't what means so much to me; it was the feeling that came with it. So I double my own enjoyment by passing that feeling along."

To Pete's amazement, his mother smiled. "Thank you, Lisa. It's a lovely birthday gift. And a nice thought," she said quietly as she put the chain around her own neck. "Passing it on," she murmured, mulling over the words as she glanced around the table at her family.

Lisa saw an opportunity to toss in another thought.

She turned and grinned at Pete. "It's the same kind of thing your son has been doing with an eager piano student in France who hero-worships him. When the boy wondered whether he could afford a lesson from the maestro here, Pete started teaching him free of any charge with the suggestion that the favor should be passed on someday."

Pete gaped at her, wondering how she knew about those lessons. He'd never mentioned them.

"In France?" Pete's father piped up. "Some kid in France wanted to be taught by my boy?"

The shocks were rolling over Pete in great, dizzying waves. Had he heard a hint of pride in his father's voice?

Lisa had realized right after arriving on the farm that Pete didn't brag about himself to his family. But she could. And how else were they to know of his accomplishments? How could he expect them to be proud of his success if they hadn't heard about it?

Several minutes later Pete cleared his throat and got to his feet. "It sure is getting late," he said with a strained smile.

"Pete, you still blush!" Addie said, laughing.

"He's done that since he was little," Peggy put in, unable to suppress a smile. "We taught him it was wrong to be boastful, but he took the lessons too much to heart."

"I say we all turn in now," Pete suggested with a note of desperation in his voice.

Addie ignored him. "Lisa, I'm so glad you've brought us up-to-date about Pete. He won't tell us a thing. But you know, he's not the only one in this family who's afraid of seeming conceited. Peggy has been asked to do up her prizewinning preserves for a gourmet shop, for instance."

"Have you, Mom?" Pete asked, surprised and yet knowing he shouldn't be. He'd seen a lot of blue ribbons come home from state and county fairs over the years.

Grinning, Addie went on as if a floodgate of pride had been opened. "And, Lisa, you should hear me trying to get Ted to admit he's been positively brilliant about helping his father modernize the farm. And then there's Pop himself: He'd die before he'd show you his hobby, but if you're interested in carvings, you just have to see the ones he does. He just calls it whittling, of course, not scrimshaw, but I swear he creates works of art." Obviously remembering that Lisa knew a lot about such things, Addie laughed with embarrassment. "At least, they seem like works of art to me."

"Pete's right," his father said, slapping his knees as he got to his feet. "We should turn in now."

Laughing, Addie dashed into the living room and brought back two wooden figures, one of a man in overalls looking down at a dog beside him, the man leaning on a shovel with one arm, his other hand scratching the dog's ear. The second carving was a woman drying her hands on her apron, a tiny smile curving her lips. Placed correctly, the two figures seemed to be looking at each other.

"You have a good eye, Addie," Lisa said as she took each carving and studied it, running her fingers over the satiny wood. They reminded her of the sculptures she'd collected in her travels. "Mr. Cochrane," she said softly to Pete's father, who was leaning against the wall looking distinctly self-conscious, "these people must be very special to you."

He frowned. "My mother and dad. The way I remember 'em from when I was a kid, not the way they got to be."

"Did they run this farm before you?" Lisa asked, seeing a bit of Pete, his brother, and his father in both the miniature wooden people she was holding.

"And their folks ran the place before them, and theirs before that," Hank answered.

"It's amazing," Lisa murmured. "I've never lived in one place more than a few years. It must be wonderful to look out at that incredible expanse of land and know that you have such deep roots in it, that you're part of a long, continuous chain." She stopped, suddenly aware that she was revealing more of her secret longings than she ever had before.

"Well, I'm not the richest man ever was," Hank said, "but this generation and the next, and—" He glanced at Addie, then looked quickly away. "And maybe even the one after that, won't be the ones to break that chain." He cleared his throat. "Lord willin', that is."

Pete stared from his father to Lisa and back again, realizing with a slight shock that his sophisticated lady and his salt-of-the-earth father had found acres of common ground.

"Seems like a nice girl," Hank said as he shook hands with Pete when the visit was over.

"That she is," Pete said with a grin, translating his father's remark as a strong suggestion not to let Lisa get away from him.

It wasn't the first time Pete had thought about making their relationship permanent. And the matter dominated his thoughts long after the poignant departure from Iowa farm country.

But when their stay in Chicago was over and he had to say good-bye to Lisa once again, Pete knew he still had to contend with a lingering seed of doubt inside him, a need to prove his worth to her—and to himself—before he could ask her to share his life.

And of the two choices facing him in his career at the moment, he wasn't sure which one would do the job.

Lisa was delighted to find that the office had run smoothly while she'd been gone. Then, when word came that her Chicago presentation had won the art gallery owners' tour for Dreamweavers, Lisa knew she was going in exactly the right direction with her management decisions. Falling in love with Pete had intensified her sense of purpose; her energy seemed boundless.

She began work on the next stage of her plans—and of Stefanie's plans for the company as a whole. "Dreamweavers, Inc. is about to become what is known, in computer jargon," Lisa said to Marie and Colette, "as a fully integrated operation. By the time this consultant we've hired has finished getting us set up, and we've all taken courses on how to work with our new state-of-the-art equipment, we'll all be so hooked up, it won't matter where we Sinclairs are, as long as we keep our little lap-top computers handy."

What Lisa still wasn't sure of was where her personal life was going. She was willing and almost ready to work out ways to spend more time with Pete. The only problem was, he hadn't asked.

She told herself again and again that Pete loved her, that for the moment he had enough decisions to make without trying to sort out the details of his love life.

But there were nights when old fears returned to haunt her, when she wondered if Pete was more satisfied with their long-distance love than he was admitting, when she even allowed the awful thought to flit across her mind that she might not be the only woman in his life.

Although Pete loved Lisa's voice, he wanted much more of her than that. Just two weeks had passed since the Chicago visit, but a lot of things had happened that he and Lisa hadn't done much talking about.

He went out for coffee with Harry Milton in New York the Thursday morning after both of them had wound up a long workweek—Pete in the recording studio, Harry in a Manhattan jazz club. "I don't want any more of this insanity of being so far from Lisa," Pete told Harry. "And I want to marry her."

"It's about time," Harry said in his teasing drawl. "But why do you sound so belligerent?"

Pete laughed. "I guess I do sound that way. But I can't seem to help it. Lisa's a successful woman, Harry. And she's still based in France, though she's mentioned that the office there is becoming pretty self-sufficient."

"So what's the problem?" Harry asked.

"Unless I make it big with my album, which is a pretty iffy proposition, I'll have to keep on hitting the road here," Pete answered. "How can I ask Lisa to trail along with me? The other alternative is for me to go to Nice, rest on the laurels I've gotten there, and forget about my ambitions for making it big in the States. I can't see myself living with Lisa as if she's some kind of patroness, but that's the way it could turn out if I don't keep pushing myself. What kind of proposal can I make under those circumstances, Harry?"

"The same kind I made to Sheila," Harry answered calmly. "The same kind lots of guys make: You tell the lady how things are, and let her make her own decision. Give Lisa some credit, kid. She cares about you, not about the status of your fame and fortune at any given time."

Pete thought about Harry's words for a while, then all at once made up his mind. He stood, went to the bank of pay phones at the far end of the diner, and used his credit card to place the long-distance call.

He hesitated when he heard the phone being picked up at the other end. What was he going to say? Why hadn't he rehearsed for a few minutes before going onstage for what might be the most important moment of his life? What kind of proposal could he make from a phone in a diner?

"Dreamweavers," he somehow heard through the blood pounding in his ears.

He couldn't speak for a moment. It wasn't Lisa's voice. "Colette?" he asked after a moment. "This is Pete. Pete Cochrane. I'm calling from New York."

"Oh, Pete, I'm sorry! Lisa isn't here right now. She had to go out to a yacht party. She'll be so disappointed to have missed your call. Is there some message I can give her? I'm on my way out to do a tour, and there's no one here but a temporary receptionist, but I could leave a note."

Pete shook his head, so deflated it didn't even occur to him that Colette couldn't see his gesture.

"Pete?" she prompted. "Are you still there?"

"I'm here," he said with a start. "There's no message. I'll catch up with Lisa later." When he went back to sit down with Harry, he said nothing, just picked up his coffee mug and drained it.

"What happened? Did Lisa turn you down?" Harry asked.

"She wasn't there. She was out at some *yacht* party," Pete answered, laughing at the way his dramatic moment had just fizzled out and wondering whose yacht Lisa was on, whose party she'd gone to.

Harry finished his coffee and got to his feet, tossing down enough money to cover the tab. "I have to be on my way or I'll miss my ride to the airport," he said, then shook his head as he grinned at Pete. "You know, I've never heard anyone make the word *yacht* sound like a curse before. Be careful, kid. Don't let your runaway pride cost you a terrific lady." With a wink and a little salute, Harry was on his way.

Pete sat staring into space for a while, then got up and strode to the phone again.

Colette had left for her tour-guiding assignment, so Pete had no choice but to ask the receptionist to put a note on Lisa's desk. Then he rushed back to his hotel, did some errands, and managed to book himself out on an overnight flight to Nice.

"She's *where*?" Pete demanded, trying not to let his ragged nerves show. But his flight to Nice had been delayed three times for a total of four hours, the plastic airline meals had been even less palatable than usual, and the stock promoter seated next to him had spent the whole night trying to rope him into at least four different once-in-a-lifetime, can't-miss deals. The last straw had been climbing the stairs to Lisa's office only to be told that she'd gone to Antibes to see her artist. *Her* artist. That was how the birdlike little brunette behind Colette's former desk had put it. "Didn't Lisa get my note? Didn't she know I was coming?" he said impatiently.

"Mademoiselle Sinclair said nothing about expecting anyone, *m'sieur*," the receptionist replied, her feathers not the least bit ruffled by Pete's minor explosion. "I know only that I put the note on her desk, and she was in her office first thing this morning, so she must have received your message."

Pete found it difficult to believe that Lisa would go off somewhere without even leaving word for him when she knew he would be arriving. But it seemed she'd done just that. "When will she be back?" he asked.

"Probably not at all today," the woman blithely answered, randomly hitting the keys of the typewriter like a child picking out dream vacation spots on a map of the world.

"I'll be sure to tell Lisa how helpful you've been," Pete said through clenched teeth.

His irony was lost on the receptionist. *"Merci, m'sieur,"* she chirped as she peered intently and proudly at the single word she'd just typed.

Pivoting on his heel, Pete strode out of the office and down the stairs. Just as he reached street level, a thought hit him. He actually struck his forehead with the heel of his hand before racing back upstairs, taking two steps at a time. He breezed past the reception desk and flung open the door to Lisa's office.

"*M'sieur,* I've told you that Mademoiselle Sinclair is not here," the receptionist protested with all the outrage she could muster.

Pete ignored her, going straight to Lisa's desk. There was no note. The wastebasket was empty. Either Lisa had gotten his message and taken it with her, or . . . "Aha!" he said triumphantly, seeing a corner of a piece of pink memo paper sticking out from a slit at the back of the rickety desk. He caught the bit of paper between his thumb and forefinger, pulled it out, and looked at it. "My message," he said with satisfaction. Lisa hadn't known he was on his way after all.

The receptionist was standing at the door with her hands on her hips, trying her best to look very cross. "Exactly who are you to be forcing your way in here?"

Pete grinned. "I'm Pete Cochrane. And I'm Lisa's fiancé, that's who," he answered, stretching the truth just a touch. "Now, about this artist of hers . . ."

"Pete Cochrane?" the woman said, her whole manner changing. "Really? You are the jazz pianist? And you're engaged to Mademoiselle Sinclair? Oh, my goodness . . . I didn't mean to imply that there's anything personal going on with that artist, Monsieur Cochrane."

Pete smiled. His Côte d'Azur renown was proving useful.

The receptionist went on hastily, "It's just that Mademoiselle Sinclair said she had to go to see this artist because he had called to say he would give lectures in his studio to certain special tour groups. It seems that she has been trying to win his consent for months, and she finally persuaded him when she had the chance to talk to him yesterday on some mutual friend's yacht. . . ."

"In Antibes, you said?" Pete asked, too impatient to listen to all the details. Antibes wasn't far. He didn't want to wait until Lisa got back to Nice. He could rent a car. "Will she be there all day, do you think?"

"No, m'sieur. She must be in Cannes by four o'clock for a meeting with the manager of a hotel used by Dreamweavers. If you wish, I can give you her entire day's itinerary. Perhaps you can catch up with her."

"Oh, yes," Pete said, grinning broadly. "I do wish. Very much."

Lisa was having trouble fighting a bit of a depression as she stepped off the elevator into the bright, airy lobby of the Cannes hotel where she'd just struck a terrific deal with the manager, pinning down preferred room rates for her clients.

She told herself she should be exhilarated. Not only had she just completed some very successful negotiations, she'd put another feather in her cap earlier in the day. She was absolutely thrilled that an artist of Paul Duroc's caliber had agreed, at long last, to do occasional lectures for the more serious art lovers among her Dreamweavers clients. And so many other things were going well: Marie was zipping through her computer course as though she had cut her teeth on a word processor, tours were being booked almost as fast as the ads for them appeared, and the new tour guides hired to keep up with the demand were working out beautifully.

The only negative Lisa could see, at least where

her business was concerned, was that she was going to have to talk to the secretarial agency about the people they'd been sending over lately. Perhaps this season was as busy as they claimed, but she was getting a little tired of having to show temporaries how to take the dustcover off the typewriter.

Yet the matter of occasional staff certainly wasn't what was bothering Lisa. What was nagging at her was that Pete hadn't made his usual phone call the night before, and when she'd tried to reach him at his New York hotel, she'd been told he'd checked out.

She didn't want to be worried. After all, she kept telling herself, Pete didn't have to report his every move to her.

Still, it wasn't like him to miss a call or to leave his hotel without saying anything.

Perhaps he'd accepted a last-minute club date, she thought. It could happen.

But why hadn't he called? Was he all right? What if . . . ?

Cool it, Lisa, she ordered herself. One missed call, and she was going into a tailspin. After being raised by parents like hers, hadn't she learned that loving someone didn't mean putting him in an emotional cage?

She was walking through the hotel lobby when the concierge stopped her. "Mademoiselle Sinclair?" the tall, very thin, very well-dressed man said, a pleasant smile softening his angular features. "Mademoiselle, one of your clients learned that you were here and wishes to buy you a drink." With a wave of his hand, he indicated the glass doorway to the hotel's pleasant little wine bar.

Lisa groaned inwardly. It was after five, and all

she wanted to do was get back home to Nice. Perhaps Pete had phoned by this time or would call during the evening.

But clients were clients. With a gracious smile, she nodded to the concierge and headed for the wine bar. One glass of Perrier, she promised herself, and she would be on her way.

A waiter met her just inside the door, nodding as he glanced over her shoulder.

Lisa looked back and saw the concierge, still standing there. She could have sworn he'd been gesticulating just as she'd turned, but he smiled sweetly at her, steepling his fingers in front of his chest like a pious pastor.

"Mademoiselle Sinclair?" the waiter asked.

Lisa nodded, deciding as she followed the man to a corner table, just past the small grand piano and behind a potted plant, that this client of hers, whoever he or she might be, must have passed around some hefty tips. She hoped the generosity sprang from an eagerness to tell her good things about Dreamweavers.

But where was this mystery person? She was the only one at the table.

"Your party will join you in a moment," the waiter explained, then snapped his fingers, almost by magic conjuring up an assistant with two champagne flutes, an ice bucket, and a bottle of Roderer Cristal.

The client had to be pleased, Lisa thought with relief. Complainers didn't, as a rule, offer the likes of Roderer Cristal.

When the waiter started opening the bottle, Lisa protested. "Shouldn't my host be here?" she asked with a smile.

"My instructions were to begin pouring as soon as

you were seated, mademoiselle," he said as he gently worked the cork from the bottle. He was just filling the glasses when Lisa's sixth sense became aroused. In the same instant, she heard the haunting, sensual sound of Duke Ellington's "Sophisticated Lady" and her eyes brimmed with sudden tears as she turned to face the piano.

Pete grinned and winked.

And an instant later the patrons of the bar were laughing and applauding the loudest and most discordant jazz chord any of them had ever heard as the pianist they had begun listening to was attacked by an amorous blond who threw her arms around his neck and kissed him passionately.

Eleven

"Wedding gift number one," Pete said as he took a small box from his pocket and handed it to Lisa, bending to capture her soft, sweet mouth in a gentle kiss. "You look so right, perched here on this wrought-iron love seat under a magnolia tree like a true Southern belle," he murmured when he'd reluctantly released her lips. "So perfect," he added, trailing his index finger along her delicate jawline, "I think I'd like to marry you tomorrow."

Lisa smiled and shifted over to make room for Pete to sit beside her, unable to speak as she found herself almost overwhelmed by the thought of being Pete's wife in less than twenty-four hours.

Pete looked around at the huge yard, lush and beautiful in the unseasonably warm early winter. "What do you say we start looking for a stately old mansion here in New Orleans, Lisa? T.J. tells me he and Stefanie looked at several places they liked before they finally settled on this one. And think how perfect a setting it'll be for that crazy office furniture of yours. Now that those pieces are being retired, they'll need a home as much as we do, don't you think?"

Lisa laughed, but felt her eyes moisten with tears. "Someday I really would love to put down roots of our own in a home like this," she managed to say, opening the package to find a velvet box. Raising the lid, she gasped and brushed back one tear that had suddenly gotten away from her. "Where did you find such a perfect present?" she whispered, almost reverently touching the enameled brooch—a miniature, chrome-yellow, hot-air balloon with a tiny rainbow curved over its side.

"I didn't find it," Pete said, taking the brooch and pinning it to the lapel of Lisa's red wool jacket. "I asked Morgan to have it made by one of the Key West artists she's always bragging about. I wanted to give you a memento of one of the most special of all the days you and I have shared . . . so far." He reached into his pocket and took out an envelope. "Wedding present number two."

"It's more like number twenty," Lisa protested. "You give me too much, Pete."

"I can't ever give you too much," he answered softly. "You're my love."

Lisa barely managed to blink back another tear.

"Besides," Pete said lightly, putting his arm around Lisa, "you already know about this gift, and it's as much from you to me as the other way around. The paper just makes it official."

Lisa unfolded the deed to the small villa she and Pete had bought in Beaulieu-sur-Mer, just outside Nice. "You do realize that we're going to have to draw up a schedule for all the relatives we've offered our villa to as a vacation spot when we're not there?"

"And don't forget our friends," Pete said with a grin. "Like Harry and Sheila, Justin and Bobby-Jo. . . . As my future wife tends to philosophize, what's the good of owning something if you can't share it with the people you love? Now," Pete said, handing Lisa another envelope, "gift number three. This is the one that means we won't have to wait until some distant day to start putting down our roots, honey. We can call a real estate agent whenever we like."

Lisa unfolded a letter from the fledgling recording company Pete had chosen to work with for his album. She read through the three short paragraphs, then read them again. And again. "It's something of a miracle," she said at last.

"You know, Lisa," Pete said quietly, "way down deep I knew all along which choice you wanted me to make when I was faced with my little professional dilemma, even though you were so careful to be noncommittal. I have to admit I was tempted to go for the money and hope to regain my integrity later, but from the moment I told you I'd decided to take the big risk instead, and you still wanted to marry me, I was sure everything was going to turn out this way."

Lisa squeezed her eyes shut. "It was your faith in yourself, Pete," she said when she'd regained control. With a shaky laugh, she added, "My goodness, what a coup! You get to keep your artistic integrity *and* have a hit album! I think I'd better stick with this corn-fed kid from Iowa I found down on Bourbon Street. He's going places!"

"Speaking of corn-fed kids from Iowa," Pete said, giving Lisa a quick hug as he got to his feet. "Wait right here. Don't move. There's still another present."

"Pete, this is getting ridiculous!" Lisa said when

he came back with a medium-size box. "You can't keep—"

"This one isn't from me," he interrupted. "It's from another corn-fed kid. My dad and I had lunch at the hotel a while ago, and he asked me to deliver this parcel to you."

With her forehead creased in puzzlement, Lisa carefully opened the package.

When she took out the carving, she gave in completely to her tears.

And when she looked at Pete, she noticed that his eyes suddenly had turned red and watery.

The figure showed a young man—obviously Pete—looking off into the distance, his head tilted back as if he were listening to music only he could hear.

"It seems," Pete said after several moments, "that I'm not the only Cochrane who loves you, Lisa."

"It also seems," she said with a smile, "that you're far more loved than you ever knew."

The media couldn't resist the wedding of the latest star on the jazz horizon to the second youngest of the beautiful Sinclair sisters. A horde of local reporters showed up, and a few from national publications as well.

The reception promised to be a colorful affair, the guest list including more well-known musicians than Bourbon Street itself could boast—and all of them bringing along their instruments for a jam session. The catering staff at the New Orleans Meridien was preparing elegant French fare along with Cajun, Creole, and soul food . . . and a steaming tub of Iowa sweet corn.

In the guest room of Stefanie's new home, Lisa's

oldest sister finished buttoning her into the white peau de soie gown that had been their mother's wedding dress.

"Where are those other two?" Lisa asked Stefanie, feigning frustration.

Stefanie laughed. "The last I saw, Morgan was out on the porch teaching Justin the finer points of arm wrestling, and Heather was in the kitchen reading your future father-in-law's palm."

With a fond shake of her head, Lisa did a pirouette, then looked at her reflection beside Stefanie's in the full-length mirror. "There's an advantage in being a squirt after all," she said with a happy smile. "I'm the only one who didn't grow taller than Mom." She loved the gown's high neckline, the long sleeves that came to a point on the backs of her hands, the seed pearl trim, the nipped-in waistline that flared out to the full skirt. Most of all, she loved knowing her mother had worn the same dress to marry the man she'd been so happy with for so long. "I feel as if wearing this gown is good luck," Lisa murmured as she turned to look at herself from several angles.

"Careful, squirt," Stefanie teased. "You're sounding like Heather."

"Well, maybe we should listen to our baby sister. Perhaps her silly talk of fate and karma and predestined love isn't as nonsensical as we'd like to think," Lisa said.

Stefanie frowned slightly, thinking. "I must admit there are times when I wonder . . ." With a laugh, she checked her smooth blond hair, then stood back to tilt her head to one side, looking critically at herself.

"Do you really like your dress?" Lisa asked anxiously, watching Stefanie's glance skim over the deep rose matron-of-honor gown Lisa had picked out. It wasn't the sort of pretty confection Stefanie would choose for herself, but it had seemed so right that Lisa had dared to ask Stefanie to wear it.

"Actually, I just love this gown," Stefanie answered, smoothing her hands over her slender waist. "It's so romantic. And in a way, it's strangely up-to-the-minute stylish. Only you could have found it, squirt." In a sudden burst of affection, Stefanie hugged Lisa and said, "It's time to get you to the church, Lisa Sinclair, so take a deep breath, because you're about to embark on the best adventure yet. Take it from your big sister; it doesn't get any more exciting than this."

Less comfortable with all the fuss than she seemed, Lisa was glad Pete kept a protective arm around her waist as the gaggle of reporters waiting outside the church tossed questions at them after the wedding.

"How do like your new in-laws?" one of them asked Pete. "The Sinclairs are quite a clan to marry into."

Smiling, Pete glanced at Lisa's sisters: Stefanie, tall and regal and as intimidating on the surface as she was softhearted inside; Morgan with her larger-than-life aura, her dazzling smile and engaging personality, her tumble of curls the color of spun apricots; Heather, the lovable red-haired minx Pete had known she'd be. He saw T.J. talking to Morgan's husband, Cole, and knew he'd formed a bond of real friendship with both men already.

And then there were Lisa's parents, Pete thought, his heart swelling with fondness and gratitude. Not only had they created the woman he adored, they were showing where Lisa had learned her sensitivity: Thanks to the warmth and thoughtfulness of Kate and Charlie Sinclair, Pete hadn't had to worry a bit about his family's feeling comfortable.

His father had summed up the Sinclairs with his usual brand of eloquence. "Lisa's folks," he'd said. "Fine people."

"Well?" the reporter prompted. "How does it feel to inherit the Sinclair family along with your lovely bride?"

Pete grinned. "How does it feel to inherit the Sinclairs?" he repeated, then hugged Lisa a little closer to him. "About the way it would feel to inherit King Solomon's mines."

"Where's the honeymoon?" another journalist asked.

Pete grinned. "It's a secret until we've left. Even from the bride. And if you know anything about these Sinclair women, you can imagine what a monumental task it was to get the lady to agree to let me keep it a secret."

The reporters laughed and allowed the couple to go on to the reception.

Hours later, when Pete finally managed to spirit Lisa away from the lively party and into the waiting limo, she laughed and nestled in his arms. "Okay, Mr. Cochrane. You said you'd tell me as soon as the wedding was over, so let's have it: Where are we going for our honeymoon?"

He kissed her before answering—a long, possessive, heart-stopping kiss. Then he smiled. "Why, Bora Bora, Mrs. Cochrane. Where else?"

Coming next month:
Heather Sinclair's love story,
the final in *The Dreamweavers* series:
BEWITCHING LADY
A March release (on sale in early February)

THE EDITOR'S CORNER

We suspect that Cupid comes to visit our Bantam offices every year when we're preparing the Valentine's Day books. It seems we're always specially inspired by the one exclusively romantic holiday in the year. And our covers next month reflect just how inspired we were ... by our authors who also must have had a visit from the chubby cherub. They shimmer with cherry-red metallic ink and are presents in and of themselves—as are the stories within. They range from naughty to very nice!

First, we bring you Suzanne Forster's marvelous **WILD CHILD**, LOVESWEPT #384. Cat D'Angelo had been the town's bad girl and Blake Wheeler its golden boy when the young assistant D.A. had sent her to the reformatory for suspected car theft. Now, ten years later, she has returned to work as a counselor to troubled kids—and to even the score with the man who had hurt her so deeply! Time had only strengthened the powerful forces that drew them together ... and Blake felt inescapable hunger for the beautiful, complicated hellcat who could drive a man to ruin—or to ecstasy. Could the love and hate Cat had held so long in her heart be fused by the fire of mutual need and finally healed by passion? We think you'll find **WILD CHILD** delicious—yet calorie free—as chocolates packaged in a red satin box!

Treat yourself to a big bouquet with Gail Douglas's *The Dreamweavers:* **BEWITCHING LADY**, LOVESWEPT #385. When the Brawny Josh Campbell who looked as if he could wield a sword as powerfully as any clansman stopped on a deserted road to give her a ride, Heather Sinclair played a mischievous Scottish lass to the hilt, beguiling the moody but fascinating man whose gaze hid inner demons ... and hinted at a dangerous passion she'd never known. Josh felt his depression lift after months of despair, but he was too cynical to succumb to this delectable minx's appeal ... or was he? A true delight!

Sweet, fresh-baked goodies galore are yours in Joan
(continued)

Elliott Pickart's **MIXED SIGNALS**, LOVESWEPT #386. Katha Logan threw herself into Vince Santini's arms, determined to rescue the rugged ex-cop from the throng of reporters outside city hall. Vince enjoyed being kidnapped by this lovely and enchanting nut who drove like a madwoman and intrigued him with her story of a crime he just *had* to investigate . . . with her as his partner! Vince believed that a man who risked his life for a living had no business falling in love. Katha knew she could cherish Vince forever if he'd let her, but playing lovers' games wasn't enough anymore. Could they learn to fly with the angels and together let their passions soar?

We give a warm, warm greeting—covered with hearts, with flowers—to a new LOVESWEPT author, but one who's not new to any of us who treasure romances. Welcome Lori Copeland, who brings us LOVESWEPT #387, **DARLING DECEIVER,** next month. Bestselling mystery writer Shae Malone returned to the sleepy town where he'd spent much of his childhood to finish his new novel, but instead of peace and quiet, he found his home invaded by a menagerie of zoo animals temporarily living next door . . . with gorgeously grown-up Harriet Whitlock! As a teenager she'd chased him relentlessly, embarrassed him with poems declaring everlasting love, but now she was an exquisite woman whose long-legged body made him burn with white-hot fire. Harri still wanted Shae with shameless abandon, but did she dare risk giving her heart again?

Your temperature may rise when you read **HEART-THROB** by Doris Parmett, LOVESWEPT #388. Hannah Morgan was bright, eager, beautiful—an enigma who filled television director Zack Matthews with impatience . . . and a sizzling hunger. The reporter in him wanted to uncover her mysteries, while the man simply wanted to gaze at her in moonlight. Hannah was prepared to work as hard as she needed to satisfy the workaholic heartbreaker . . . until her impossibly virile boss crumbled her defenses with tenderness and ignited a hunger she'd never expected to feel again. Was she

(continued)

willing to fight to keep her man? Don't miss this sparkling jewel of a love story. A true Valentine's Day present.

For a great finish to a special month, don't miss Judy Gill's **STARGAZER,** LOVESWEPT #389, a romance that shines with the message of the power of love . . . at any age. As the helicopter hovered above her, Kathy M'Gonigle gazed with wonder at her heroic rescuer, but stormy-eyed Gabe Fowler was furious at how close she'd come to drowning in the sudden flood—and shocked at the joy he felt at touching her again! Years before, he'd made her burn with desire, but she'd been too young and he too restless to settle down. Now destiny had brought them both home. Could the man who put the stars in her eyes conquer the past and promise her forever?

All our books—well, their authors wish they could promise you forever. That's not possible, but authors and staff can wish you wonderful romance reading.

Now it is my great pleasure to give you one more Valentine's gift—namely, to reintroduce you to our Susann Brailey, now Senior Editor, who will grace these pages in the future with her fresh and enthusiastic words. But don't think for a minute that you're getting rid of me! I'll be here—along with the rest of the staff—doing the very best to bring you wonderful love stories all year long.

As I have told you many times in the past, I wish you peace, joy, and the best of all things—the love of family and friends.

Carolyn Nichols

Carolyn Nichols
Editor
LOVESWEPT
Bantam Books
666 Fifth Avenue
New York, NY 10103

Joni Clayton

It's really great fun to be a LOVESWEPT Fan of the Month as it provides me with the opportunity to publicly thank Carolyn Nichols, Bantam Books, and some of my favorite authors: Sandra Brown, Iris Johansen, Kay Hooper, Fayrene Preston, Helen Mittermeyer and Deborah Smith (to name only a few!).

My good friend, Mary, first introduced me to romance fiction and LOVESWEPTS in 1984 as an escape from the pressures of my job. Almost immediately my associates noticed the difference in my disposition and attitude and questioned the reason for the change. They all wanted to thank LOVESWEPT!

It did not take me long to discover that most romance series were inconsistent in quality and were not always to my liking—but not LOVESWEPT. I have thoroughly enjoyed each and every volume. All were "keepers" . . . so of course I wanted to own the entire series. I enlisted the aid of friends and used book dealers. Presto! The series was complete! As soon as LOVESWEPT was offered through the mail, I subscribed and have never missed a copy!

I have since retired from the "hurly-burly" of the working world and finally have the time to start to reread all of my LOVESWEPT "keepers."

To Carolyn, all of the authors, and the LOVESWEPT staff—Thanks for making my retirement so enjoyable!

60 Minutes to a Better, More Beautiful You!

Now it's easier than ever to awaken your sensuality, stay slim forever—even make yourself irresistible. With Bantam's bestselling subliminal audio tapes, you're only 60 minutes away from a better, more beautiful you!

__	45004-2	**Slim Forever**	$8.95
__	45112-X	**Awaken Your Sensuality**	$7.95
__	45081-6	**You're Irresistible**	$7.95
__	45035-2	**Stop Smoking Forever**	$8.95
__	45130-8	**Develop Your Intuition**	$7.95
__	45022-0	**Positively Change Your Life**	$8.95
__	45154-5	**Get What You Want**	$7.95
__	45041-7	**Stress Free Forever**	$7.95
__	45106-5	**Get a Good Night's Sleep**	$7.95
__	45094-8	**Improve Your Concentration**	$7.95
__	45172-3	**Develop A Perfect Memory**	$8.95

THE DELANEY DYNASTY

Men and women whose loves an passions are so glorious
it takes many great romance novels by three bestselling
authors to tell their tempestuous stories.

THE SHAMROCK TRINITY

☐ 21975   **RAFE, THE MAVERICK**
by Kay Hooper   **$2.95**

☐ 21976   **YORK, THE RENEGADE**
by Iris Johansen   **$2.95**

☐ 21977   **BURKE, THE KINGPIN**
by Fayrene Preston   **$2.95**

THE DELANEYS OF KILLAROO

☐ 21872   **ADELAIDE, THE ENCHANTRESS**
by Kay Hooper   **$2.75**

☐ 21873   **MATILDA, THE ADVENTURESS**
by Iris Johansen   **$2.75**

☐ 21874   **SYDNEY, THE TEMPTRESS**
by Fayrene Preston   **$2.75**

THE DELANEYS: *The Untamed Years*

☐ 21899   **GOLDEN FLAMES** *by Kay Hooper*   **$3.50**

☐ 21898   **WILD SILVER** *by Iris Johansen*   **$3.50**

☐ 21897   **COPPER FIRE** *by Fayrene Preston*   **$3.50**

Buy them at your local bookstore or use this page to order.

Bantam Books, Dept. SW7, 414 East Golf Road, Des Plaines, IL 60016

Please send me the items I have checked above. I am enclosing $_____
(please add $2.00 to cover postage and handling). Send check or money
order, no cash or C.O.D.s please.

Mr/Ms _____

Address _____

City/State _____ Zip _____

Please allow four to six weeks for delivery.

SW7—11/89

Prices and availability subject to change without notice.

NEW!

Handsome Book Covers Specially Designed To Fit Loveswept Books

Our new French Calf Vinyl book covers come in a set of three great colors—royal blue, scarlet red and kachina green.

Each 7" × 9½" book cover has two deep vertical pockets, a handy sewn-in bookmark, and is soil and scratch resistant.

To order your set, use the form below.